The Book of Right and Wrong

The Book of Right and Wrong

Matt Debenham

THE OHIO STATE UNIVERSITY PRESS / COLUMBUS

Library of Congress Cataloging-in-Publication Data

Debenham, Matt, 1970–
  The book of right and wrong / Matt Debenham.
      p. cm.
   ISBN 978-0-8142-5173-7 (pbk. : alk. paper)—ISBN 978-0-8142-9225-9 (cd) 1. Short stories,
American. I. Title.
   PS3604.E2335B66 2010
   813'.6—dc22

This book is available in the following editions:
Paper (ISBN 978-0-8142-5173-7)
CD-ROM (ISBN 978-0-8142-9225-9)

Cover design by Dan O'Dair
Text design by Juliet Williams
Type set in ITC New Baskerville
Printed by Versa Press, Inc.

♾ The paper used in this publication meets the minimum requirements of the American
National Standard for Information Sciences—Permanence of Paper for Printed Library
Materials. ANSI Z39.48-1992.

9 8 7 6 5 4 3 2 1

Contents

Acknowledgments

Skip this page if you don't know me personally. You'll be bored!

The following stories were originally published, in different forms, in the following places: "Depot Island," *North Atlantic Review;* "Still Life with Dead Bird," *Dogwood;* "Beard of Bees," *Painted Bride Quarterly* and *Weston Magazine;* "I Was Jimmy Carter," *Weston Magazine;* "Kate the Destroyer," *The Pinch;* "The Book of Right and Wrong," *Roanoke Review.*

I'd like to thank my friends and teachers from the Bennington Writing Seminars, the Sewanee Writers' Conference, the Fine Arts Work Center, and Gotham Writers' Workshop. In particular: Eric Raymond, Emily Bloch, Chad Simpson, Marsha McSpadden, Mary Otis, Amy Greene, and Jane Ransom. Thanks also to the Connecticut Commission on Culture and Tourism for financial support.

These stories wouldn't have been possible without the love, encouragement, and kindness of my parents, Roger and Karen Debenham, and my mother-in-law, Donna St.Onge.

This book is for Caissie and Eli and Lincoln.

Beard of Bees

Try not to think of the bees as stinging you, I tell my son. Think of them as snuffling. Like a dog would do!

"But it hurts," says Jasper. His eyes still hold the last of his tears. The real waterworks are only minutes gone, the boundless, shameless wailing of a six-year-old.

"Okay, well, to them you're a giant flower," I say. "You like flowers, right? Pretend that."

"I won't!" he yells. "It *hurts!*"

"Your mother used to complain the same way when you were at her boob, by the way. 'Ow, he's biting me!' she'd say. But you know what? Mom stuck with it. She didn't run away from *you*."

"But she's run away now," he says.

"Yes, but not because of you."

"I miss mom already," says Jasper. "How come she left us?"

Try not to think of Mom as having left, I tell him. Think of us as staying put. Like a dog would do.

If I say I miss her, then the terrorist has won.

* * *

When the bees came, they did not come in swarms. They came in crates. Unfortunately for me, they also came while I was at work. My wife Gayle was home, though, and signed for them, thinking they were the frozen steaks I was supposed to have ordered. Then she put them in the coffin-sized ice-chest in the garage and stacked the four old snow tires back on the filthy white lid.

Those were the first bees.

The second batch I had sent to my work. In hindsight—I teach 4th grade—this probably wasn't the best idea. Ms. Gaultieri, our secretary, came hustling into my classroom and whispered, through a strained grin, "Mr. Baron, your *packages* are here."

"Oh, great!" I said. "I'll pick them up at the end of the day."

"No," she said. "There's something wrong with them. They're *crackling.*"

"Oh, that's just the bees. They're fine."

Three minutes later the principal pulled me out of my classroom. She didn't even pretend to smile for the kids.

"You had *bees* sent to an elementary school?" she hissed. "Are you out of your head, man?"

"I wanted them to be safe," I said. "You should see what my wife did to the other shipment."

"In my office, Mr. Baron, do you know what's hanging on the wall?"

Principal Riddick is thirty and wears boxy black suits every day to go with her spiky black hair. She has a PhD and used to work in advertising. There's some talk about her sexuality, though I notice that's usually among the people here who are the furthest past thirty and who don't even have master's degrees. Me, I respect anyone who's been through a graduate program. I could never have stood that much school.

"There are pictures of two dozen children on the wall next to my desk," she says. "The severe-allergy kids. I need to know their faces in case something goes wrong while they're under my watch. Do you know the life-threatening allergy that twenty of them have in common?"

I indicated that I did not.

"Beestings."

"Jeez, really?" I said. I'd been sure she was going to say peanuts. "So, what then, you have to use those pen-things on them?" I was genuinely curious. Unfortunately, I also then made a motion like I was plunging a needle into her chest, and she took a sharp step back.

"Just get that *shit* out of the building," she said. Behind me, the room burst into giggles. "Miss Riddick said the S-H-I-T word!" someone yelled. More laughter, some shrieks.

The principal turned white and looked like she wanted to swallow herself from the inside. I felt for her. Every educator remembers his first time being pinned, helpless, by the laughter, or silence, of children.

"I'll pull my car around back," I said. My son's classroom was in the front. I very much didn't want him seeing what suddenly struck me as a weird and shameful act, like I was loading up my car with mail-order pornography.

As easy as it would be to blame the bees, I refuse. Obviously the problems were deeper. They had to be: Was our marriage really built on some unspoken vow that we'd live a bee-free life together? When Jasper and I showed up after school that day in the Hyundai full of bees, the thing Gayle said to us was, "This is not what I signed up for." Which, in hindsight, seems less like a complaint than a pox. She didn't take Jasper with her, she didn't ask for a divorce. She just went, leaving that phrase behind for us to enjoy in her absence. We eat our breakfasts with it, sleep with it, share our showers with it. It's been a long spring for the left-behind.

Jasper won't be in my grade for another three years, but I keep an eye on him throughout the day via Kelly Bargain, his first-grade teacher. Kelly is about five minutes out of college, chubby-cute, with blond corkscrew hair and that impossibly wide smile all new teachers wear, the one that breaks the hearts of the rest of us. One afternoon in May, she tells me Jasper's been painting some troubling scenes in the Creative Expression Lab.

"Can I see?" I say.

She wrinkles her nose and shakes her head. "I wouldn't if I were you," she says. "Though I think he's advanced for his age. When his people are chopping with axes? They really stand as if they're chopping."

That night I invite my dad and his third wife down for the weekend. It takes every ounce of strength I have. Even though we're not close, I figure it'll be good for Jasper to have some extra family around to help plug the Mom-hole.

Turns out I did the right thing, inviting them. Friday afternoon, only hours before they're due at the house, Kelly Bargain reports more worrisome activity.

"Your son's pretty into this one girl," she says. "Annabelle." It's lunchtime and we're sitting side-by-side on the front of my desk.

"Yeah, Jasper's never done the whole girls-are-icky thing," I say. "Heredity, I guess." I add this with a slight lift of my left brow. It's feeble, I know, but I could use the practice.

She giggles: Apparently I was being ironic. "Anyway," she says. "Today he told her he'd kill for her."

I swallow. "That's sweet, in its way."

"Then he asked her how many heads of his enemies it would take before she'd agree to be his concubine."

As a parent, you can keep your failings secret, bury them at home under piles of dishes and ill-chosen arguments, but they will always burrow their way out and find you, always in your most brittle public moments. Heads of enemies, concubines: It's all my doing. Gayle used to read him *Go, Dog, Go!* and *Stuart Little* at bedtime. In the weeks since she left, I've been reading him things I thought were more boyish, in hopes of kick-starting the masculine bond between us. We just finished *Conan the Barbarian.* Some of it really stuck with Jasper, apparently. Maybe now I'll hold off on the Raymond Chandler. I'll admit, I've been having a little trouble with some of the less tangible aspects of parenting. I do remember being really good at diapers.

"John?" says Kelly Bargain. She's never used my first name before. Or any name, I realize. Usually she just comes up very close and starts talking as if she'd just turned away a minute ago. Six months ago, a trait like this might have annoyed the crap out of me. Now it's a huge turn-on. How low does a person have to get before enthusiasm qualifies as an aphrodisiac?

"Yes, Kelly?"

"What's with the bees?"

"Ah. You heard."

"I heard."

It's as if Gayle is watching me from some other dimension. *Yeah, John, what* is *with the bees?* Never mind that I haven't touched them since she left.

"To make a beard," I say. This is the reason I gave Jasper for getting the bees; maybe Kelly will be as excited as he was. "Who wouldn't want a beard of bees?"

Kelly laughs, so I laugh with her: Of course! We're kidding!

"Really, so what's the whole deal?" says Kelly Bargain. "You have, like, a special suit and everything?"

"Just gloves and a bonnet." *Somewhere,* I think. "Why? Would you like to see them?"

She smiles. Then she nudges my thigh with hers. "I think I'd like to see you *in* them."

And I think: Gayle who?

When Jasper and I get home from school, my dad and his third wife are waiting for us on the front porch.

"You're early," I tell them.

"We peed on the bushes out back," says my father, rising to shake my hand.

"It was a double emergency," says his third wife. Okay, her name's Lottie. She's a permed, perfumed expanse of a woman. Whenever I see her, I experience a feeling of queasy dissonance, and then I realize it's because she looks like she could be my mother's older sister. "I watered the hostas while Lou did the Rose of Sharon," says Lottie. "Jasper, do you have a hug and a kiss for your grandmother?"

Jasper gives me a look—*Have I met this person?*—before letting himself disappear into the front of her dress.

We get them inside, dump their luggage in my former bedroom—after Gayle, the couch became my fort—and proceed to sit in the living room and stare at each other politely for a quarter of an hour. In between, my father looks intently out the window, as if he's spotted a really interesting squirrel. Lottie hums to herself and smoothes her dress across her thighs.

Finally, Jasper says, "Oh, hey. We got bees!"

Lottie points a finger at me. "You call someone about that, pronto. Once you see one, you know there's dozens more, probably."

"Or thousands," I say. I wink at Jasper.

"Eh?" says Lottie.

"They sting like hell," says Jasper.

"Hey!" I bark. He recoils. My father remains looking elsewhere, but his ears have gone red. Lottie pats the cushion next to her leg, and Jasper crawls right up next to her. I remain in my seat, feeling spineless and mean.

You don't get a third wife, of course, without having driven off two others first. And this is not counting the ones my father dated in between, the ones who smelled bad electrical and didn't wait around for the black smoke to start showing up. Whatever he did, I apparently took good notes—and then threw them out. I mean, *bees?* As they say in the kung-fu movies I'm no longer going to let Jasper watch, the student is now the master.

My dad and Lottie nap, then we all go to Pizzeria Uno for dinner. As we walk in, Lottie says, "How about that? There's a place near us named this, too."

I open my mouth, but my father's already glaring at me, shaking his head with short, violent strokes.

After we've ordered, I ask them how their nap was.

"Splendid," says Lottie. She pats my father's arm. "This man was born to spoon."

"Anyhow," says my dad, quickly. I wonder why you would marry someone like Lottie, then, if you were someone like my dad. But then, I've been feeling unbalanced myself since we sat down, as if I'm in a car with the wrong-sized tires on one side. And then I get it: Jasper, who's next to me now, was across from me the last time we ate in a restaurant as a family, and every time before that. But now, beside me, he's too little to fill the spot where the other person used to go.

"What should we do tonight?" says Lottie. "Paint the town red?"

Jasper cups his hands over my ear and whispers: "Can you do the trick for them? The beard?" He really means for him, too, since I haven't actually ever done the trick. Nor do I really want to. Then I remember: Kelly Bargain is coming by later. Our cover story is that she's returning some drawing that's incredibly important to Jasper. Then, after he falls asleep, we're escaping my dad and Lottie and going to a movie. But what Kelly Bargain really wants to see is a beard of bees, I can tell. And suddenly I'm willing to risk injury or death. After all, if I survive, it might make the rest of the night really good.

Finally, I whisper to Jasper all the words he is allowed to say about it.

"We have something truly amazing planned for you," he tells them in his best MC's voice. "An after-dinner show. And that's all I'm saying."

"Well, now," says Lottie. She makes an expression that's a mix of impressed and curious, a hard thing to do without looking patronizing.

It's funny how other people can make you like your children more. Maybe sometimes you need to be reminded, Hey, got a good kid there. Or maybe it's that you realize how little you think of them as anything but question-machines, sleep-stealers. When the waitress comes back,

I order Jasper a hot-fudge sundae. No one says anything about the absent woman.

Back home, Jasper and I lead them to the bees. The hive boxes are stacked at the far edge of our property, where the low stone wall abuts the old dairy farm next door. Jasper's all wired up on sundae-power. In the dusk, the fudge smeared around his mouth looks like what Jasper says is the blood of the vanquished. I make a note to find *Charlotte's Web* when we get in. He whirls around sloppily, hacking at the long grass with a bald, brittle stick.

"Wowie zowie," says Lottie.

While Jasper does his Barbarian thing, I watch my dad walk along beside the wall, inspecting the colonial craftsmanship. Every now and then he'll pat a stone, maybe to see if it wobbles, maybe for encouragement.

The beard trick? Hold the queen between your lips. That's it! Or so I've read. Bees will blindly go wherever the queen goes. That's all they know to do. If you've got a hive box full of bees and the queen dies, you have to replace her right away. Otherwise, the whole hive falls apart: The field bees won't know anymore to go out and get pollen or nectar, and the workers won't know to keep producing honey. Thousands of little beings starving to death, all because one is missing.

I think I can pull off the beard trick. I'm just trying to think of how to get them all back into the hive without getting myself sent to the hospital. I make a note to look it up online before I go luring them out.

"Aargh!" yells Jasper, and I look up to see him leap onto my dad, pointy stick still in hand. He's crept along the top of the wall just to ambush the old man. I cringe, picturing me at six, doing this to my dad. But instead the old man laughs and lets Jasper ride him crashing to the ground. Jasper tosses his weapon aside and pretends to eat his grandfather's face. Lottie shouts encouragements. When he finally stands up, they're both wearing the sundae-fudge of the vanquished.

Lottie turns to me. "You're awful quiet."

"I'm expecting someone," I say, not looking at her. "A friend."

"Oh," she says. Then she looks at me. "Oh! Well, isn't that nice?"

"Maybe. You don't think it's too soon? Jasper kind of knows her."

Lottie shrugs. "My husband was in the ground a month when I met your dad. If you could time these things better, you would. But you shouldn't."

I suddenly want her to crush me in a perfumed hug. More than that, I want to tell her things, want to grind my tears into her matronly shoulder. But why, though? Why this person I fail to recognize every time we meet? My wife used to say I was like a bad driver of my own emotions. "You'll cry over the dog you lost at 16," she'd say, "but not at our son's birth. Or you'll stew for days over a 30-second political commercial, but you won't give 30 seconds' thought about why someone might be unhappy all the time."

In the end, I just tell Lottie she's probably right, that you can't mess with fate. Then I excuse myself to go inside while Jasper and my dad trade barbaric growls.

I have the telephone handset in my fingers, ready to cancel on Kelly Bargain. I'm getting the bullet points down: *Bad timing . . . difficult days ahead . . . try again later maybe? Really was looking forward to this.* And she may be her usual understanding self, maybe even continue the flirtation. Eventually, she'll drift away from me in school, fall for some substitute gym teacher, making me regret ever making this call. But the fact is, it really *isn't* time to start liking/loving/driving-off someone new. It's time to be around Jasper more. Time to be fixing things at home.

Outside Lottie is laughing and shrieking. The copper smoker device sits on the kitchen counter, packed with tightly rolled cardboard for a slow burn, ready to subdue some bees so I can reach in and get to the queen. A thought comes rolling along: The queen is identifiable by a dot on her back—but how am I going to see this in the dusk? The phone rings in my hand.

"Hey," says Gayle. My wife. I can hear traffic in the background. She could be two miles away, or in New Delhi. She sounds warbly, nervous. "I left a message earlier. You didn't get it? I thought maybe you guys hit the road and joined the circus. Ha-ha! Anyway, I just wanted to check in and let you know where I've—"

And here her words get swallowed by the screams from outside, much louder than before. Through the kitchen window I see my dad and Jasper still rolling around on the ground. I should yell out the window, tell Jasper that's too hard. Clouds of dust swirl around them, a dark, busy dust. On the handset, Gayle chatters along. Lottie is running back and forth now, waving her hands like she's putting out a fire. She's okay, that Lottie, a good sport. Then a chunking sound from the side of the house—a car door—and I see Kelly Bargain running across my lawn, toward my crazy little family. Boy, she's a game one. Maybe I should give it a chance. I thought I'd fall apart when Gayle finally called, but as it happens, I haven't heard a thing she's said; all her little words have been swallowed up by the sound of my family. Right now everyone's calling my name. It's nice to be wanted.

Then I see the hive boxes, tipped and splayed on the ground. The pointy stick lies across them. An angry little cloud hangs in the air. Beneath the cloud, my dad is on all fours, vomiting in the grass. Kelly and Lottie are hauling Jasper along by his arms, the whites of his sneakers flashing in sleepy, rhythmless steps. He has his own little cloud, floating around his head.

And in the phone, my wife says, "Anyway, what about you, John? Are you a new man yet?"

Still Life with Dead Bird

New Year's Eve, two minutes till midnight, walking the new Corgi. My wife the doctor was at work. She'd switched with someone for the shift.

The dog had come to us from the same litter as one belonging to a woman I'd been seeing at my own work. We were winding down as a thing, but then she got this perverse idea of us both having sibling dogs. Being an art professor—sorry, *assistant* art professor—this woman apparently had no choice but to name her pup Whistler. She claimed it was because he was a boy, and because he was the one who tottered forward when she whistled into the kennel crate, but come on. So I announced that I was thinking of naming my dog Whistler's Bitch Sister. *Exeunt professor.* I liked the name, though, so it stuck, sort of. My wife called the dog WBS for short. Or so I'd read: She worked sixteen-hour days, mostly nights; I worked at the university, regular-human hours. We communicated by Post-Its. Not the ideal media, but I'd never gotten around to learning computers, and I'd learned long ago that telephone contact with an emergency room doctor was only slightly more reliable than a séance. lots of not-quite-there in this p

Anyway, the New Year's snow in the streetlights looked like a gown of gauze and sparkle falling endlessly to the floor.

Whistler's Bitch Sister and I had just turned the corner onto Pleas-

how would he
explain the name
to his wife?

ant Street when I spotted someone else out with his dog. The person was bent over a snow bank beneath a huge black oak. At first, I thought he was vomiting: New Year's and all. But when I got closer, I saw a) he was a woman; and b) she was examining something in the snow.

"Whatcha got there?" I said. She jumped. Her dog, a bony little bug-eyed thing in a dark green sweater, rasped and lunged at me. Whistler's Bitch Sister concealed herself behind my legs.

The woman was tallish, with a pointy nose and small, dark eyes. She was bundled in a long, dirty-pink tube of a coat, a scarf that hid her neck and chin, and a stripy pom-pom hat. When I asked what she had there, she shook her head in the way of a recent immigrant. This being Worcester, it wasn't out of the question.

"Sorry," I said. "Español?"

She rolled her eyes and pulled her scarf away from her neck. I looked, then looked again. There was a stubby plastic nozzle in her throat. That couldn't be right. She was probably ten or twelve years younger than me, still tucked safely in her thirties. I'd only seen these things on old men. But there it was, pointing at me like the barrel of a rifle.

"From cigarettes?" I said, then mimed it by puffing between two fingers. In case she still didn't speaka de ingles.

She shook her head, then put a gloved finger over the end of the tracheotomy tube. There was a soft sucking sound, followed by a phlegmy, guttural croak. "Steering wheel."

"Jesus Christ," I said. "Don't do that again."

I should probably state here that most adults find me kind of insen-sitive. My college students, of course, can't get enough of it. Mostly they love the swearing, the slanderous remarks about my fellow faculty, the stories about James and Nora Joyce's colorful sex life. (I teach American lit, but I like the kids to know the full range of my know-how.) Then finals hit and they realize they haven't learned much about literature, American or otherwise, from good old Professor Crispin.

The woman's finger went to the trache tube again. "Sorry," she belched. Then: "Won't speak again." Then: "A thousand apologies for your discomfort. I sure hope it hasn't been too awful for you."

Hardy har. I began to say as much, then stopped. She'd moved aside enough for me to see what she'd been looking at when I came along. It was a frozen bird, a Chickadee, lying on its side in the snow bank. It was perfect and bloodless, like a Christmas ornament.

I turned to the woman. Minus the nozzle, she was pretty, in a rough, long-jawed way. In a Worcester way. Despite all the literary evidence against dead birds as positive developments, I gave her a smile. Then I asked if I could walk with her.

When I got home, there was a message from my wife on the machine.

"Professor Crispy," she said. "Don't forget to take that dog of yours out for a walk. Notice I said walk, Crisp, not smoke. I know it's New Year's, but don't give in. And don't smoke the dog either. That's just a little—oops! Gotta go. GSW in the H-E-A-D. Love you, see you next year." Beep.

The next night, the woman was waiting under the tree. Same dead-bird time, same dead-bird channel. Only now, someone had added a tiny green pear next to the Chickadee, as if just out of reach of the beak. On the other side, apparently for symmetry, lay a complete zipper torn from someone's jeans.

"Everyone's an artist these days," I said.

She handed me a note. *won't be talking to-nite. still hurts somedays. I'm Maxene. like the andrews sister. dog is Batshit.*

The four of us walked, picking up a comfortable rhythm with each other. Since Maxene's throat was bothering her, I took it upon myself to carry the conversational slack. Work, my classes, how our fair city of Worcester—central Massachusetts in general—was beyond saving. The standard Crispin-walks-with-woman patter. Not that I knew where we were headed, figuratively speaking. The nozzle, the sexless coat: This was a woman I could have introduced to my wife. And yet.

I was raconteuring along through a Faulkner-in-Hollywood story when Maxene whacked me in the arm. I looked over and she stuck a note in my face. It said: *I was hoping You could not talk also.*

I read this a few times, trying to remember when she'd pulled out a pen.

"Wait," I said. "Did you write this in advance?"

She smiled sweetly, then tapped the note with a stern finger.

Up I clammed.

I should probably state right here that no children were harmed during the making of this episode. There are no Professor Crispin Juniors running amok. Which was more my wife's decision. It's true I never stated a preference either way, but I feel I should point out what's what here. People always assume it's the man.

The voice is a little too wry and cynical for me to
really go along with. Seems too obviously constructed

Still Life with Dead Bird   13

The lady of the house is named Sherry, like the drink. I *wish* she'd drink. Then I'd have an excuse to feel so put-upon. Instead, I married an ER doctor, for Christ's sake, one who regularly covers day shifts in pediatric triage because she "likes to feel useful." Hers was the first name listed on our mortgage; those extra shifts bought me the vehicle I'm embarrassed to park in the faculty lot next to the Geos and Hyundais. Hard to feel oppressed by all that, but somehow I manage. A man, a dog, an empty fridge: Cue the strings.

Maxene and I met every night that week. Midnight, under the big, black oak with Batshit and Whistler's Bitch Sister, no chit-chat. The bird was there, too, along with the zipper. The pear lasted only a night before some animal carried it off in its jaws.

It was stupid, I know, shitting where I ate. I should have been worried about being seen, someone calling my wife, said wife coming home sick from work. But all I could worry about was whether Maxene would be at the tree when I got there. What we were doing still wasn't clear to me. We hadn't so much as touched hands, never mind spoken, since the first night. And yet, she had my full attention. There's something about the intimacy of walking alongside someone, especially someone you know nearly nothing about. The fact that we hadn't done things made it even more exciting. It meant we were doing *nearly* nothing, but not quite. I assumed she was married, though she never took off the gloves. I didn't know if she had kids, a job, how long she'd lived in Worcester.

I hoped I'd never see her in the daytime. In the dark, where the world has shut itself away, you pick your companions as carefully as you would your sounds. We floated together in secret waters, Maxene and I. Daytime was too bright, too loud, too dry. I could see why my wife liked working the late shift.

The next Sunday was our one-week anniversary of whatever this was. I felt like I should buy her flowers or something, but I restrained myself. Instead, I bought her a card.

She walked us to the street lamp and opened it there. As she wrestled with the envelope, the scarf fell away from her throat. I looked away, but it was too late: Where my eyes went next, the trache went with them. Earlier in the week we'd had a warm spell that melted a third of the snow, and there was fog all around our little cone of light. I half-expected a werewolf or mummy to come staggering out of the billows.

Instead, a car passed us. It slowed, brake lights bruising the fog. My feet went cold. We'd been nailed. Was it my wife? There was part of me that hoped so. *This is what it looks like,* I wanted to tell the good doctor. *This is two people together.* What I wanted the reaction, or the result, to be, I couldn't have told you. I looked at Maxene, but she was reading the card. When I looked back up, the headlights had vanished, and I could hear the car climbing the hill, away from us.

Maxene was smiling when I turned back. She had the card held tight to her chest and shook her head slowly in that way that doesn't mean no. She pulled me against her and took my gloved hand in hers. In our little megaphone of lamplight, we rocked back and forth like seventh-graders at a dance. The dogs settled in furry parentheses around our feet. After a minute of this, I felt Maxene's jaw moving against mine. At first I thought she was chewing gum. I drew my face back a little, and in the corner of my eye, I could see Maxene's lips moving. She was singing.

The next day I woke up late. The pillow next to me smelled of recent wife. I was nearly sick with guilt. I hadn't slept with someone who wasn't my wife, hadn't even kissed another woman. Yet I felt worse than the times I actually had done those things. At the same time, my cheek felt cold. It missed its companion.

Downstairs, there was a note impaled on my car key.

Crispy Critter, it said. *If you could just fix the snoring, you'd be the best roommate I ever had. Do you miss me? Check this box, yes or no. Seriously, give me a call at work sometime. Let me know what you're thinking about these days. Literature? Civic planning? Divorce? Har-har.*

My late-morning class was an abortion, with me off my usual game and my students curiously interested in hearing some ideas, since it was clear the laughs wouldn't be forthcoming. Lunchtime found me down the street at Mulcahey's, enjoying a lunch of hops while the rain fell like a box of needles from the sky. I was alone at the bar, watching the TV newsbreak. A sugar truck had jackknifed on the Pike. It looked like an honest mistake when the reporter said there were no cavities, instead of no casualties. A knee brushed mine as someone slid onto the next stool over.

"Rolling Rock?" the man said. The bartender, a big Irish gal I've seen for years but have never known by name, slid a green bottle past me.

"Thanks," said the man. "She's married, you know."

I thought this an odd thing to say to one's bartender, but I was in no position to judge.

The man spoke again. "I said, 'She's married, you know.'" I turned to look at the guy, who was glaring up at me. He was no one I knew: short brown hair, caterpillar mustache, froggy eyes. In his brown-framed glasses and light blue sweater, he looked like a high-school computer teacher.

"How long, pal?" he said. His feet dangled and kicked arrhythmically at the chrome legs of the stool. It sort of undermined any menace he was trying to project.

"How long what?" I said. I'd had similar exchanges before at Mulcahey's. Lots of non-sequiturs, people starting conversations at the midpoint. With the college squatting in a bad part of town, the nearby bars attracted an interesting element, particularly in the daytime.

"You and Maxene," he said. My blood froze. "I saw you from my car last night." He nodded. "Oh yeah."

In the fog of my mind, taillights flashed. "I don't know what you're referring to," I said. I sipped at my beer, hoping I looked nonchalant.

"Isn't it 'to what you're referring?'" he said. "You're not much of an English teacher, are you?"

I almost told him I taught American literature, but then I realized he'd just identified me as a teacher. Had Maxene told him?

"We haven't done anything," I said. Then I pictured the two of us in his headlights and I knew this was the worst lie I'd ever told. We humans spend all our time after junior high trying to get laid, but is there anything more intimate than two people slow-dancing together?

"So," he said. "You know about the throat yet?" Something like giddiness flickered in his eyes.

"How could I not?"

"No, smartass. I mean, what'd she tell you about it?"

I picked at the label on my beer and shook my head.

He smiled. His teeth were shaped like corn niblets, and his lips were bitten raw. "Ho, buddy," he chuckled, and he toasted me with his Rolling Rock.

I waited for him to elaborate, but he didn't, just kept staring ahead. Finally, I gave in. "Well?"

"I'm just fucking with you," he said. "But see? You wondered, didn't you? You thought maybe there was some dark story behind the trache. Did you want to hear a dark story, professor?"

I wondered how Maxene had filled him in about me: verbally, or in note form?

"Here's a good one," he said, and he began to tell me.

A man waits at home for his wife to get back from the restaurant she manages—the one she manages to come home from later and later every night. He falls asleep on the couch, wakes up with the phone ringing. It's 3:23 A.M. and St. Vincent's is on the line. A woman with ID indicating this address has been involved in an accident, and he needs to come down immediately. They won't tell him any more than that. He backs out of the driveway so fast that he kills his neighbor's cat. Only later, but every time after, will he hear the sound of the tiny skull against his rear axle.

At the hospital, they tell him the woman's alive, but she's got a crushed throat and a broken pelvis, some internal bruising. He thinks, My wife, the seatbelt Nazi? The pretty young nurse says they're working on her right now. Then she says, So did they call you down because you're related to the husband or the wife?

The man says, I *am* the husband.

The pretty young nurse says, Well, wait. Then who's the guy they brought in with her? That's when an older nurse appears and sweeps the young nurse away.

Her husband stopped there. "You like that story? Make you feel closer to her?"

I didn't know what to say to that.

"Ever pack a wound? Drain a tracheotomy?"

I stood up to go.

"You're wasting your time, professor. She can't do what you're looking for anyway."

That stopped me. "Which is what, exactly?"

"*You* know. It's too painful. They had to reconstruct her. She's probably still part steering column, for all I know." He laughed mirthlessly. "And yet! It's worse than death, apparently, for her to sit in the house with me for an entire night!"

I bent down to where he was still sitting. "I'm really sorry," I said.

He chuckled and held up his hands as if to say, *What are you gonna do?* Then he spit in my face. We stared at each other a second—there was no shoving, no halfhearted raising of fists—and then I walked away, leaving him with the bar to himself. It seemed I owed him that.

some good things in the scene, but the husband is also overdone.

* * *

Five before midnight in my living room, I stand up to go. My raincoat's on, the dog harnessed. I don't know what I'm doing. Maxene won't be there. Or she will be, and then we'll really be in it, unable to plead any sort of ignorance or innocence. We'll run off together somewhere and discover more bad qualities in each other. Or we'll keep going like this, circling the neighborhood night after night, until the husband snaps and kills himself. Or her, or me, or all of us.

The phone rings, and the machine picks up. I stand over it as my wife begins speaking. I go for the receiver, but the sight of my shaking fingers stops me. I can do messages, but not conversations. "Hey there," says my wife of twenty years, and they're the two most beautiful notes I've ever heard sung. "I actually came home around noon today, had the whole rest of the day off. I figured when you came home, we could go out, sit at a table together, eat some food, talk some talk. Then I got called back in. One of these days, I'll have to learn how to say no." She says she hopes I'm eating right, am brushing and flossing and using pleasant language with people.

For the last hour I've been picturing my wife working on some patient in a curtained-off bed the night Maxene and her friend were brought in. I didn't want to imagine the rest: whether they crossed paths or not, whether my wife ever had her fingers inside Maxene's throat. Or another possible scenario: Maxene on the gurney, opening her purpled eyes just long enough to see the pretty, sad-mouthed doctor disappear into the napping room with some tall young resident.

On the machine, the pretty, sad-mouthed doctor is still talking. She's musing now about the time we won't spend together this weekend: rounds, paperwork, a staff-only luncheon. Then her voice is cut off with a bright electronic chirp: end of message space. My heart breaks at the sound. I think of the pristine bird corpse under the oak, framed by the pear and the torn clothing. In the thrill of finding such a weird display, I'd forgotten to consider how the bird might have died in the first place. Did it jump or was it pushed?

I'm supposed to reveal how much my wife means to me, paint in tiny strokes a series of scenes demonstrating why I would still care about her after all we have (or haven't) done to each other. Truth is, at this point I can't remember. All I know is once upon a time she planted a sliver in my heart, and the tissue grew around it. Having it removed, even by the hands of an expert, might kill me. This, I realize, must be why people have babies: multiple slivers, yes, but harder to distinguish individual pain. Kind of like the old gag of stomping on the guy's foot to distract him from his headache. Is that why you never meet a depressed Mormon?

I bend down to grab up the dog's leash, but it's not there; Whistler's Bitch Sister has gotten bored and wandered off to another room, leash in tow. Dogs love babies, don't they? I can picture her padding up, tentatively, and snuffling that small, warm head, the little swirl of chick-fur hair. Even the whining and crying would be a nice change from the grown-up version. It's a terrible idea, of course. Still, how many more nights can Maxene's husband and I keep sitting in empty houses? And how many more people can it possibly take to keep emptying them?

I Was Jimmy Carter

Miles LaPine was Jimmy Carter. Jeffrey Tunxis was Ronald Reagan. He was also the most popular boy in the fifth grade. No one else seemed to remember he'd wet his pants when they were all six. They had no trouble remembering Miles' supposed past as a booger-eater. The Reagan team even used it in their posters for the mock elections: *Why Pick Carter When He Can Just Pick Himself?*

The feeling was, you couldn't be too careful where the Reagan kids were concerned. From the start, they'd showed they were willing to go further, chalking PEANUT FARMER GO HOME across the kickball diamond. In the middle of October, they'd tripped a girl from the Carter campaign in the lunchroom. They'd even given a head-flushing to one of their own, a guy who'd snitched to the vice principal about some of the threats that were going around. Rumor had it that the boys on Team Reagan had mobbed the dart booth at the Autumn Festival. Supposedly, they'd stolen a bunch of Nunchuks and kung-fu "butterfly" knives when the hippie carnival worker was taking a smoke break. The Lake Street School principal clearly had no idea what he was doing when he suggested the fifth grade try a fun exercise in democracy.

Miles' father was thrilled that his son was going to be Jimmy Carter.

At dinner that first night, he'd pulled Miles' chair closer to his, kept nudging him lovingly.

"The Man from Plains," he said, pointing at Miles. Carrie, Miles' older sister, rolled her eyes. Their mother, who had a clear handle on the national mood that election year, just looked worried.

Miles' father had been campaigning for Carter all year in their part of Massachusetts. Even after getting a beer can in the back of the head and a pair of Dobermans sicced on him, the man's heart was still with Jimmy Carter and the Democratic party.

"So, Miles?" Mr. LaPine said. "How'd you get it? Stirring oration? Nominated by your peers?"

This was how: Miles had been in his seat, daydreaming about elves and Orcs, when Lisa Carmody whispered, "Raise your hand, dummy!" And when he did, he was the president no one wanted anymore.

"Nominated by peers," he told his dad.

Later, with just the two of them at the kitchen table, Mr. LaPine grilled him on strategy.

"Who's your Reagan?" he began.

"Jeffrey Tunxis."

"Bill Tunxis' kid? Lord. Does the kid have his own construction company yet?"

His dad hated Bill Tunxis, seemingly for the giant pickup trucks he drove around town. Because of the gas shortage, the LaPines had traded their station wagon for a tiny used Datsun whose seats smelled of ruined diapers. Miles' dad was very proud of this sacrifice, and couldn't seem to let a large-sized car pass without comment. The Tunxis family still roared around town in their Bronco, which was big enough to carry the Datsun, plus groceries.

"Crap, I'm sorry," said Mr. LaPine. "Don't let your mother know I said that stuff. Is the kid at least smart? Dynamic? Inspiring?"

Miles thought about it. "He's got the only pair of leather Nikes in school."

His dad shook his head. But he was smiling. "Okay," he said. "A guy can't win on footwear. Now, if that's the attribute he's known for, I would say this thing's yours to lose. The world is thirsty for integrity. That's why Jimmy Carter is still the man for America, and it's why Miles LaPine is the man for Lake Street School."

But Miles was somewhere else, still stuck on the shoes. Jeffrey's were big and white, like cars on his feet, and they squeaked when he walked. Miles held up his own shoes: crappy fake Converse from the sneaker factory in East Brookfield, with canvas the color of old gauze. The rubber had come unwrapped from around the toe. It looked like a dirty tongue, razzing him from the end of his own foot.

"The Man from Plains," his father said again, fake-punching Miles in the arm.

"Thanks, Dad."

Tonight's newspaper lay between them on the table. In black and white, Ronald Reagan waved from the front page. To Miles, he looked like a nice enough old guy. Mr. LaPine poked the paper with his finger. "Wait till our man wipes the smug look off that old bastard's face."

School Election Day in 1980 was a Friday, October 31: Halloween. The national election would happen the following Tuesday. The principal wanted the fifth-grade version to be done by then so they'd have something to compare theirs to. It was all part of Democracy in Action week.

Miles woke up early to get himself ready. He was on his feet at 4:30, putting on his church shirt and slacks. Then he went outside and threw himself around on the ground for a few minutes. When he was finished, his shirt was ripped and smeared with dirt. He'd add the fake blood stains later, as if he'd been feasting on human prey. Election Day or no, it was still Halloween, and he was going to school dressed as the Wolfman.

In the yard, he collected clumps of brown grass. He had it sticking out of the pockets and cuffs of his slacks, to show he'd been writhing in pain during his horrific transformation. His inspiration was *Abbott and Costello Meet Frankenstein,* which was the best monster movie of all time because in addition to the titular monster, it also featured Dracula *and* the Wolfman (and even an end cameo from the Invisible Man). It had been on the Boston UHF station two Saturdays ago. The Wolfman wasn't really the main monster in the movie, but to Miles, he had the showiest role.

Lon Chaney Jr. is in his room, trying to keep himself together despite the inevitability of the lunar cycle. Suddenly, we see the clouds sliding apart. There's a full moon behind them. Then it's back to Lon Chaney Jr., who's now screaming and tossing himself around, as if he were on fire inside. Thick hair crawls up the backs of his hands, and when he stands up again, he's the Wolfman.

It was a great scene, but it also made Miles a little sad. What if he never became a cool monster himself? What if he stayed exactly the same person all his life? Good little Miles, reformed nose-picker, *Hobbit*-reader, the only person at the book discussion meetings the school librarian insisted on holding every week. The Man from Plains.

When Miles came back inside, his mother was up, too. She followed him to the bathroom and sat on the edge of the tub, watching him get ready, tapping the ashes of her wake-up cigarette over the drain-hole. Miles reread the instructions in his monster-makeup book, then coated his face with corn syrup and applied tufts of cotton. When all the fur was in place on his face and hands, Mrs. LaPine got out her makeup and put dark streaks in the fur and blackened the tip of Miles' nose. Then she wet a comb with baby oil and slicked back his hair to blend the edges of the fuzz into it. When they were done, she leaned back and smiled. "Lon Chaney Jr., Jr.," she said.

Mr. LaPine came down during breakfast. He stopped and scowled at Miles, looking over the new, furry head of his presidential candidate. "Okay," he said. "Here's how we're going to use this. Everyone says Carter's weak, right? Too passive and ineffectual? So what you say is, *Like a full moon, national crises will arise with certain regularity. And like the Wolfman, you can expect* this *president to transform at those times into a strong, instinctive presence.*" Mrs. LaPine muttered something into her coffee mug. Her husband ignored her. "Do you want to write any of that down?" he asked Miles. "Do you need me to repeat it?"

"Isn't the Wolfman kind of out-of-control?" Miles said. "Wouldn't he just leap around the United Nations, ripping out people's throats?"

His dad blinked at him with a weariness he normally reserved for Jehovah's Witnesses, or for his students. "What I said last night about integrity," he said. "Stick with that. The world, thirsty for integrity."

At school, everyone was dressed as someone or something else. Miles thought it should be like that every day. Jeffrey Tunxis came as Ronald Reagan, which made Miles feel like a moron. It hadn't occurred to him to dress as the guy he was supposed to be. Jeffrey Tunxis had on the dark blue suit, the white shirt, the red tie. His dark hair was both puffy and wet-looking. His mother, or someone, had drawn lines onto his cheeks to make him look old. As soon as he walked, though, your eyes went right to his feet. He was wearing his big, bright Nikes. Even Miles wanted to vote for him.

After morning announcements and first period social studies, they held the presidential debate from a desk on the cafeteria stage. The

there's no way he'll pull this off, it'll be the worst part of an already unconvincing story

Reagan kids took up the middle section of the room, the Carter people filling out the edges. Principal Fortunato was moderator. He read from a mimeographed sheet of questions: How would you handle the hostage crisis? What's to be done about the Soviet Union? Miles and Jeffrey Tunxis were supposed to trade responses, sliding the school's old, pickle-shaped microphone back and forth on its heavy base.

Things weren't going well. Everything Jeffrey Tunxis said got big applause, while Miles' words—his father's words—seemed to disappear off the lip of the stage. He was halfway through his third rebuttal when Principal Fortunato leaned in. "You have to push the button to talk, President Werewolf." Everyone laughed at that one.

Using the microphone right didn't really help Miles. Jeffrey Tunxis hammered away, blaming Miles for the hostages, saying Egypt and Israel were distractions. He said the number one job was keeping America secure and profitable. Miles didn't know Mr. Tunxis, but guessed he'd probably said these same things the night before. He knew whose words came out of his own mouth whenever it was his turn to speak.

Miles said Mr. Reagan sounded mainly interested in getting everyone blown up, and that his compassion seemed reserved for people who were white. He glanced at the crowd, realizing he didn't know anyone who wasn't white. no 5ᵗʰ grader would know how to say this (even in repetition)

Finally the principal cleared his throat and gave the one-minute sign. Jeffrey Tunxis leaned in and said, "Okay, well, in closing, ladies and gentlemen, just ask yourselfs: Are you better off than you were four years ago?" He waited, still clutching the little pole between the microphone and its base. Even the teachers were clapping and grinning. There was a pounding sound from beneath the table. Miles hunched down and saw Jeffrey Tunxis' big sneakers clomping on the stage. They sounded like horses galloping to battle.

When the noise had died down, Tunxis pressed the talk button again and said, "Well, Mr. President? *Are* they?" and slid the mike back to Miles.

It wasn't fair. Miles had already read most of the *Lord of the Rings,* and he was going to lose to a kid who was still mouthing his way through Encyclopedia Brown? And then there it was, a precious, horrifying memory: Jeffrey Tunxis walking sidestep out of Mrs. Harlowe's first-grade classroom. His cheeks were pink and wet, and his red-plaid pants were dark at the crotch and down both legs. Miles could still see the puddle in the shallow bowl of Tunxis' wooden seat. There was no way he was the only one who could still remember this. His dad popped into his mind, too, but Miles pushed him right back out. If Jimmy Carter had a chance to win, what would it matter how it happened?

Miles pressed the button and said, "Well, Governor Reagan, that's a tough one. But I do know this: Someone on this stage is a lot *drier* than he was four years ago."

Miles had been expecting some laughter, maybe clapping. But *nothing*. Had he forgotten to press the button again? No: Across the table, Jeffrey Tunxis' eyes were huge. After a long moment, one of the Carter kids yelled "Whoo!" and then there was pandemonium, shouting and laughing. A couple of Reagan kids stood up and made fists at the Carters.

Principal Fortunato appeared beside Miles. "Debate's over," he snapped, and grabbed the microphone from his hand. The principal lifted the mike to his mouth and said, "Recess, people. Elections after lunch."

When they got outside, the Reagan kids were already standing shoulder to shoulder. George Bush was at the front, dressed as Bruce Lee. Miles didn't see Jeffrey Tunxis anywhere, but plenty of his friends saw Miles. Their whole line stepped forward. Suddenly, people from his own side shoved past, and his back went cold, as if he were suddenly shirtless. He was being abandoned, no question. Then Miles watched in amazement as Walter Mondale, dressed in an orange bathrobe as Hong Kong Fooey, walked over and swung her foot up into George Bush's crotch.

The playground went crazy, everyone fighting in their costumes. Superman wrestled Dracula, while Daisy Duke punched the Monopoly Man. One half of some yellow fuzzy dice stood in the center of the kickball court, hands on either side of her yellow-painted face. She was howling for her other die, the one Miles had just seen whipping some kid with his bright yellow rope.

They'd all been worried about the kung-fu weapons the Reagan kids were said to have, but Miles didn't see any. It also didn't seem to matter, as Reagan people were fighting Reagan people and Carter people were fighting Carter people. It was a free-for-all. The two teachers on recess duty were overwhelmed. Miles watched them standing there, just turning and looking everywhere, hands on their faces, as if they didn't know where to start, or how. Miles thought of his father, how disappointed he'd be to hear about the debate and the follow-up melee. Then Miles stuck his foot out to trip a Reagan girl dressed like a crayon.

Miles broke his first bone, a ring finger, punching a boy he'd once gone to camp with. Someone else broke her wooden ruler across the back of Miles' neck. Later, in the mirror, he'd find a dark red stripe. Another person tore a handful of fur off his cheek, leaving a patch of skin that stung in the chilly autumn air. He realized he must look like half-Wolfman, half-president. It didn't matter: He felt like all-Wolfman.

Miles was at the far end of the playground when he saw Jeffrey Tunxis step out the side door. For a long while he just stood there, one foot still raised in step, gawking at the scene. Miles turned around, hoping to blend into the chaos. When he turned again to look, Tunxis had his back to him. He was standing over a Rubik's Cube, kicking holes in the painted cardboard while a pair of red and green legs bucked at the bottom of the costume. Tunxis' white, white sneakers made beautiful blurs as they hammered away at the Cube.

Someone had left a lunchbox by the edge of the kickball diamond. It was metal, the kind no one but nerds carried anymore. Miles snatched it up, scraping his knuckles on the asphalt curb, and began to run toward Jeffrey Tunxis.

Ronald Reagan went down as soon as that metal box hit his head. The Wolfman went down, too, falling on top of him as if he'd been hit from somewhere. Miles hoped it looked like that, anyway. Then he got to work tearing the white Nikes from Jeffrey Tunxis' sweaty feet. The other boy was very quiet and still. There was a little line of blood in front of his ear. Miles thought for a second about tasting it, just to see. Then Tunxis groaned a little, and Miles went back to getting the leather sneakers off Tunxis and onto himself.

There was no way the school could hold the elections now; democracy had chosen another venue. Miles pictured the real Carter sitting on the real Reagan, pounding him on television. Wouldn't his dad like that? Hadn't he wanted to wipe the smug look off the old bastard's face? When Miles grew up, he thought, maybe that's how it would be: no pretend-talking, no pretend-listening. You would do whatever you had to, to get whatever you wanted. You'd just come up and kick it out of the other guy's hands. It was how the Carter people would come to rule the Earth, thought Miles, how the concerned history teachers of the world would come to ride in enormous vehicles and look down on everyone else.

Little Liars

They were in the hot, rotting chicken coop at the abandoned farm down the street from Miles LaPine's house. Miles was going over his recent discoveries about *Columbia,* the new space shuttle.

"There," said Miles. He dabbed his pinky at a tiny white dot on one of the cone-shaped thrusters at the rear of the craft.

"Yeah?" said Kurt. He was thirteen, two years older than Miles.

Miles stared at him. "Can't you see it?" He seemed to actually be shaking in his seat. "God, you're no better than those fools at NASA."

Kurt drew back a fist. "Watch it, gaylord." He faked a rabbit punch; Miles flinched. Order restored, Kurt looked at the photo again. "I think that's just some shit on the film or something. Like when you go see a movie on the first night and it still has those amoeba-looking things that pop on the screen?"

Miles glanced at the shuttle picture. "Certainly one possibility," he said. He let out a dramatic breath. "But what if you're wrong?"

Miles, Kurt had learned, wrote to NASA every week. In return, he had a bedroom full of informational packets from the Agency. (Miles always called it the Agency.) Glossy sheets detailing the history of the Mercury rocket program; signed pictures from astronauts like Michael Collins, the Apollo 11 guy (the only one who *didn't* walk on the moon that first trip); and, in the newest packet, black-and-white 8-by-10s of the space shuttle *Columbia*.

"I hope they actually read my letter this time, instead of just sending me more packets," said Miles. "*Columbia*'s the one, so to miss a big hole like that? Total disaster."

"Wait," said Kurt. "I thought *Enterprise* was the space shuttle. Didn't you tell me it could fly across country in eight minutes?"

Miles rolled his eyes. "No, see, they've flown *Enterprise* and everything, but it'll never go to space. *Columbia*'s the one for the job. Though not if they continue to ignore my warnings."

He was just talking to himself at this point. Kurt lay back on the bench and closed his eyes, trying to ignore Miles and the smell of chicken shit from long-dead chickens. It was like being *inside* a chicken. And it was every day now, this queer-bait hanging-around with Miles. What if someone saw them together? What if Miles showed up at the high school where Kurt was starting in September, looking for his big buddy? What if Kurt had to really hit him then, just to keep the order of things looking right?

"You eating over again tonight?" said Miles.

Oh, but for now, there was dinner at the LaPine house.

Mr. LaPine, a high-school teacher, was out somewhere. Miles' older sister was at the movies with Kurt's older sister. That left just Kurt, Miles, and Mrs. LaPine in the big kitchen, which was nearly like it being just Kurt and Mrs. LaPine. Which was how it was supposed to be.

She'd made pigs-in-blankets, but Kurt could barely eat one. They looked like sunburned baby legs in doughy diapers. He made sure to ask for thirds of coleslaw, though.

Mrs. LaPine was younger than most moms, and she always called Kurt "Curtis," even though his name was just Kurt. Tonight she wore a pale blue tank-top so thin Kurt couldn't look at her while she was talking to him. She kept a bottle of wine up on the counter next to the table. She'd placed it just out of reach, so she had to stand and stretch over the stools every time she needed a refill. After watching her do this four times, Kurt wondered why she wouldn't just put the bottle on the table.

"Where's dad tonight?" said Miles.

Mrs. LaPine took a swallow of her wine. "He's finishing up at summer school." She flashed Kurt a half-smile. "And how's your family doing, Curtis?"

Miles' dad was what Kurt's sister and her high-school friends called a "fox." Even his mother used to joke around about getting dolled up for parent-teacher night with Mr. LaPine. Kurt's dad never seemed to care for that joke.

"My sister had summer school last year," said Kurt. "I don't think she ever came home later than four."

Miles and Mrs. LaPine looked at him, and he felt the room grow heavy. He needed to say something now, throw a lid on the boiling pot. Turning to Mrs. LaPine, he went with the first thing that came to mind. "Miles made an important discovery, he thinks."

"Ixnay!" hissed Miles. He glared at Kurt and mouthed, "That's *secret*!"

Kurt had wanted to sound grown-up, as if he were a teacher praising her son for her. But Mrs. LaPine just shook her head as if they were both speaking German. As if he were just a crazy little kid, like her Miles.

The screen door opened and Miles' dad appeared at the far end of the kitchen. He was sweaty and carried a leather briefcase and a folded corduroy jacket. His light-brown hair looked wet, and his cheeks were burnt. Kurt had seen him on better nights. He certainly didn't look like the guy his sister and her friends all mooned over.

"Guys," said Miles' dad. He nodded down at Mrs. LaPine. "Lady. Sorry I'm late." He set his things on one of the stools by the counter. His eyes moved all over the room, as if he were following a fly. Then he seemed to suddenly notice Kurt. He made finger-guns at him. "Curtis Mayfield!" he said. He looked as if he were genuinely glad to see someone extra sitting in his kitchen. He moved past the group, heading for the stairs.

"How about a kiss?" said Mrs. LaPine.

Miles' dad froze. He had one foot on the ground, and he hopped around on it to face the table, revealing a wild grin. Miles laughed. Kurt looked at Miles' mother. She was beautiful, like fresh hot sand. Who would resist, even for a second?

"This," said Miles' dad, standing normal again, "is not a human being you want to kiss right now." He touched his damp shirt and twisted his face. "Dis-gusting." Watching him touch the shirt, Kurt could see there was something wrong with it, but couldn't figure out what.

"I don't mind sweatiness," said Mrs. LaPine. "Come to the table." If Kurt's mother had said this to his father, she'd be smiling, teasing. Mrs. LaPine wasn't smiling, and she wasn't asking.

Miles' dad took a backwards step toward the stairs. "Really, though.

The window in my classroom was stuck shut all day, thank you custodian Deevers. And then during the car ride home, the needle was heading for Overheat, so I had to run the hot air the whole way here." He exhaled with the effort of his talking. "Hence, sweatiness. I'm going to shower now, and then I'll give you kisses. With interest."

Mrs. LaPine smoothed her napkin across her lap. "Or you could pay now, with no interest. Come join us."

He lingered there a moment, watching that fly again. Kurt realized what was wrong with the shirt: It was buttoned wrong, leaving one side longer than the other. Miles' dad kissed his hand and blew toward Mrs. LaPine. She lunged in her chair, as if she might catch the kiss between her teeth. But she held herself there, between standing and sitting, and instead just sniffed the air, loudly.

Miles' dad turned pale and smiled weakly at all of them.

Mrs. LaPine sat back down in her seat and took a gentle sip of her wine. Behind Kurt, heavy footsteps climbed the stairs. The table was quiet a moment as they sat and listened to the sound of shoes hitting the floor overhead.

"So, Miles, tell me about this discovery," said Mrs. LaPine. "Is it scientific? You know I love science." She grinned at Kurt. "So much happening in the microscopic world."

"Mm, well, this is bigger than microscopic, believe me," said Miles, and he was off and chattering about the hole in the space shuttle engine, the possibility of the thrusters just falling off right above Earth.

Kurt watched as Mrs. LaPine nodded and smiled at her son. He waited for her to look over at him, toss him a wink or roll her eyes like she often did, but she didn't do that this time. Instead, she just listened to Miles. Upstairs, something like a belt clanked against the other side of the ceiling.

It was heartbreaking, watching her give serious attention to crazy Miles. Kurt wanted to tell her, *He lies all the time, do you know that? Your son, the little liar. He told me one time he has a new motorcycle waiting for him when he turns sixteen. He says he's a genius. Well, what kind of genius sits in a rotten chicken coop all day, just making up crazy shit to tell himself? Do you see what I go through to be near you?*

He caught himself mouthing this last part. Had she seen him? No: She was still looking at Miles, still smiling so patiently and nodding. She looked happy to believe his crap. Kurt tuned out the words and ate his coleslaw, while above them came the sound of Mr. LaPine dropping his change all over the floor.

oh, what a cop-out! He actually had a story up and running this time

Version

I'd never pictured myself the type to kidnap my own children, yet here we all were together, driving past the city where the kids now lived with their mother. Until early that morning, my two sons and I had been having our visitation where we always did, at my mother and stepfather's house in northern New Hampshire. I'd been living there the past few years, getting my life together after the divorce that had flattened me like hot metal. When you're the parent the kids don't live with, your identity is no longer yours. Before the divorce, you could be the World's Greatest Dad, as the t-shirt says. After the humiliation, accusation, litigation, negotiation, and separation, you're down to being a frayed little strand from that t-shirt: World's Greatest Thread. You couldn't blame your children for not recognizing or appreciating the new you.

My boys, nine-year-old Noel and five-year-old Daniel, rode in my backseat. It was early afternoon, and they'd both just awakened from a long nap. The car was on the New Jersey Turnpike. Still early in the plan, such as it was: no inkling yet for the children that their father might be taking them anywhere but back to Mom and Manhattan. Kids can adapt to anything, is what my mother was always telling me, and I supposed if anyone would know that, it was the former Amelia Davis.

* * *

July, 1966: My mother and father are driving toward downtown Orlando. Their names are Amelia and Wick Davis. They're on their way to visit Amelia's sister, Ruth. Ruth's husband is stationed at the nearby Air Force base, but they live in-town, close to Lake Eola Park. Amelia and Wick have known each other since the second grade. Grown-up Wick is a construction manager in Pittsburgh—not the Pittsburgh of now, but the Pittsburgh of 1966. They have a new white Thunderbird convertible, one of two symbols of their growing success in the world. The other is parked in Amelia's womb: Fat with a restless, squirming baby, Amelia has made the trip to her sister's house against her doctor's advice.

It's a hot, sunny day and they crawl through the still Orlando air, trying to find the cottage Ruth and Gary have rented downtown, the one that's supposed to be just off the park. Then the sun goes out and they look up to see something huge and dark hurtling toward them. Amelia screams. She thinks meteor; Wick thinks Cape Canaveral. They stop the car in the middle of the street, waiting for the thing to overtake them.

But it doesn't. Instead, the commercial airplane plunges diagonal into a neighborhood just across the narrow park. It impacts with a force that ripples the trees. It kills every sound on earth for a long moment. Then Amelia realizes: Wick has thrown himself on top of her. She pulls herself from underneath his bulk and puts a hand to her stomach. The seat beneath her is soaked.

Wick shakes off the shock and notices her hand, then the darkened sundress. He says, "Are you o—" and then a car slams them from behind.

We passed the exit for the Goethals Bridge. The Goethals could have taken us to Staten Island, and was thus the last link between the New Jersey side of the Hudson and the collective boroughs of New York City. The final destination, as far as I had worked it out, would be Royal, Tennessee, the home of Mike and Patty, college friends of mine. Mike and Patty knew we were coming but didn't yet know we'd be staying. They'd never liked my ex-wife, Claire, so I was sure they wouldn't do anything to wreck things, not right away.

Meanwhile, I was still searching for a way to tell the boys about the change in their plans. I'd always taken a different route every time I dropped off the kids from visitation, just for variety, so there was no question among them yet about where they were and why. But Noel was born with my sense of direction, and it wouldn't be long before the boy realized we weren't where we should be.

This visitation had been a longer one than usual: My ex-wife was on her honeymoon with her new husband, a hedge-fund manager named Rafe. The kids had attended the wedding, against my initial wishes. Claire and Rafe had initially agreed to hold off on a honeymoon—money never takes a holiday, don't you know—but at the last minute, the newlyweds had decided, yes, they wanted a week in paradise before starting their new life together. (Though, if you wanted to be technical about it, they'd started their new life together before Husband #1 had known his old one was done.) As always, I had driven down to pick up the boys. It was a long trip, 300 miles each way, but I prized the car-time: six hours alone on the way down, sans mother and stepfather; six hours with my boys on the way back. The only bad part of the ride was the drive back to New Hampshire after dropping the kids off in the city. Then I'd get to puzzling over the last time I'd done anything right in my life, and it would be like driving home in the dark with a flashlight shining in my face the whole way.

This most recent pickup, the one before the honeymoon, I had just packed the kids into the car outside their new Broome Street address when Claire pulled me aside.

"So, Martin," said Claire.

"So, Suddenly Wealthy," I said.

"Ha. Listen, when I get back, you and I need to talk."

"We're talking now, aren't we?"

She made her pretty mouth into a pretty line; it was business time. "Okay," said Claire. "Rafe wants to adopt the kids."

I put a hand on the hood of the car, to keep from sliding to the pavement. The inside of my nose tingled, as if I'd been punched. Beneath me, the vehicle rocked as Noel and Daniel either wrestled or danced in their seats. "Am I dead?" I said. "Is this like one of those movies where the guy doesn't realize till the end that he's been dead the whole time and now it's time to let go?"

She laughed, a genuine laugh. It was, strangely, a welcome sound at the moment. "You'd still be their natural father," she said. "No one can take that away from you."

"You seem willing to try," I said. And still, I wanted my hands in her hair, the warmth of her scalp against my fingertips, those slender lips mashed into mine.

"Just, it's so hard on kids when there's that lack of clarity about parental roles." Then she added, "Believe it or not, I'm trying to save them from what you went through."

Years earlier, when we'd just met, I'd told her the story of my parents' accident. I'd first been told the story, in confidence, by my Aunt Ruth, when I was sixteen. This, of course, only compounded the tragedy of the tale—a fact I was all too aware of. When I had first told it to Claire, it was as a way of melting her heart, as a way of distinguishing myself from the hordes of young Manhattan professionals who were also trying to get into her pants. Now, after turning back time and correcting her life by marrying one of those professionals, Claire had returned to the present wise enough to work her ex-husband's own story against him.

"Well played, Mr. Bond," said I.

The Malibu moves the Thunderbird forward 20 feet until they stop sideways in the street. Wick Davis is dead. No, not dead, bloody and breathing, with a crater in the front of his head. The steering wheel is wrecked. The other driver goes to a nearby house to get help. The ambulance takes twenty minutes to arrive. When it comes, it comes from across the park, from the direction of the downed airliner. At the hospital, they wheel Amelia Davis one way and her husband another.

"Where are all the crash victims?" Amelia says.

"That's what we were wondering," the nurse says. Amelia looks up in time to see the paramedic shaking his head sternly at the nurse. During her four days in the hospital, the only people Amelia will see related to the crash are a pair of firefighters who'd injured themselves on the wreckage. Later, she will learn that all 182 passengers and crew died in the plane. Ruth and Gary, Amelia's sister and brother-in-law, come to visit: Amelia had called for them upon waking to find she'd had a son, whom she'd named Martin, after Wick's father. Ruth and Gary return every day, along with their own baby girl, Martin's cousin Andrea.

Wick is fine. His head is wrapped. The doctors had had some small concerns the first day, but he is fine. The only damage on the Thunderbird, incredibly, is to its rear fender, and to the steering wheel. The latter is bent, as if with a sledgehammer. Still: easily replaceable, all of it. Amelia uses the word miracle. Wick says lucky. Wick takes his wife and son, and they finally go to Ruth and Gary's house. The afternoon that follows is one of the finest in Amelia's life. She and her husband and baby were nearly killed a block away, and now here they are, as if merely waylaid a moment. Wick does not remember the car crash, but everyone, including Amelia, marvels as he tells about the DC-8 cutting slantways across the sky. He describes the Delta insignia, a red-

white-and-blue triangle on the tail fin. The portside wing had been on fire,
Wick could see it perfectly now, a bouquet of orange ribbons flapping behind
the engines.

"I'm hungry," said little Daniel.

"I'm bored," said Noel. "Are we in Kansas or what?" Apparently, the flat Jersey marshland running alongside the highway said "heartland" to him. Which was nice, I guess: To me, it said "final resting place of mobsters and informants."

"Believe it or not, we're not so far from civilization," I told them.

"I miss the city," said Noel. "All this land is kind of creeping me out."

"Can we stop and buy some corn?" said Daniel.

It's amazing how you can make two people from the same exact pairs of DNA, yet they'll turn out so differently. Noel, all arms and nose, was nine going on thirty, a child so much more comfortable talking with grownups than with kids his own age. Daniel, Mr. Pudgy with the big eyes, didn't have the verbal facility Noel'd had at this age, but he was so much better at *being a kid*, at holding on to the wonder and, yes, the ignorance so vital to believing the world was a magical place and not a terrifying shithole.

If I could be anyone, I would be Daniel.

"I'm gonna tell you a story now," I said. "It's not really a nice story, but you deserve to know where your dad comes from, because of course that is also the story of where you come from, and why the three of us are here now."

"What do you mean 'why the three of us are here now'?" said Noel.

"Time to zip it!" I sang, and then I told them their story, starting with the car crash in Florida.

Amelia's sister, Ruth, awakes to a clattering from the front of the house. It's
late, the end of the long day of their big reunion. Silverware jangles, plastic
cups skitter and tumble. Ruth creeps out from her bedroom, checks the babies
on the way, then rounds the corner into the bright, lighted kitchen. Wick is
there, naked, a puddle at his feet. He's going through the knife drawer.

Ruth runs to the back of the house. Her screaming wakes everyone: her
husband, Amelia, the babies. Something like hell surges through the house
as Gary tries to subdue Wick while everyone else huddles behind a cracked,

unlockable bedroom door. Finally, Wick is down, the police have been called, and the kitchen is a bloody mess.

At the hospital, the nurses seem agitated to see Wick again. They avoid eye contact, as if he is bad luck. After a few days, he is transferred to a psychiatric facility back in Pittsburgh. Amelia and baby Martin return home, too, on a different plane.

In Pittsburgh, Wick does not get better. Amelia goes to see him every day. They meet in a room where Wick's wrists are strapped to a chair and a tall, crew-cut orderly watches over everything with a boredom Amelia finds infuriating. Wick's hands are dotted with cigarette burns. Amelia does not dare ask about them in front of the orderly. She has brought baby Martin to this meeting. As Amelia catches Wick up on neighborhood news, her husband squints and scowls at the baby on her lap. Finally, he interrupts his wife. "Very nice work," he says. "Now take off its head and let's see that goddamn microphone."

The kids were quiet when I finished, and I was careful not to break the silence. I wanted to preserve the delicate membrane that had formed around them now that they'd finally heard Dad's story away from all the distractions of the grandparents' house and the ugly mechanics of visitation. Let the details ride with us a while, I thought. Let them fill the empty spaces in the car. It was as though we'd taken on a new passenger and no one was quite sure what to say yet.

Then Noel said, "You know, Mom told us that story already."

It was like being hit in the face with a rock: You smell the blood before it even comes out of you.

"She did not," I said.

"She did," Noel said. Then he smiled, the bastard. Daniel, for his part, was looking out the window as if expecting a naked man with a knife to come striding up alongside the moving car. He was still in the story, and for that I—momentarily—loved him more.

All the same, I was thinking I should have taken them by plane. A car ride, yes, kept you off the grid; but it also gave you too much time to think and talk and second-guess.

"When did she tell you my story?" I asked Noel.

"I wish we had a dog with us right now," said Daniel. "Or a gun."

Noel shrugged. "Most recently? Last weekend." He turned to the window, searching the scrubby scenery. "At the rehearsal dinner. Rafe's mom and dad came up from Florida for the wedding, so Mom said,

'Wow, I know this crazy story about Florida.'" Noel nodded, satisfied that this was the correct memory. "I've heard it from her a couple times before that." He caught my look in the mirror and his eyes widened with something like fear. "You added a lot more cool details in your version, though. In Mom's, the crazy guy didn't pee himself."

My lips were hot, and my teeth felt like little nubs of chalk. "The 'crazy guy' was my *dad,* your real grandfather," I told Noel. "Did Mom's version include how I didn't know until I was sixteen why Grandpa never hugged me or told me he loved me?" My voice was rising, hoarsening, but I couldn't stop it; it was a broken engine, accelerating on its own. "That's kind of late to learn such important information, don't you think? Do you boys know how lucky you are to have a father who loves you? Do you know HOW THE FUCK MUCH I LOVE YOU?" I caught myself screaming these last words into their reflection, a pair of already small faces shrunk even tinier by the narrow mirror. Noel looked out the window, working his jaw muscles. And then Daniel began to cry.

The next time Amelia comes to visit Wick, she comes alone. She sits down in front of Wick and crosses her legs. He looks at her, and she scoots her chair back, just a little. Wick says, Get us a divorce. Sell the car if you have to. Don't ever come back. Don't let that little boy see me again. He still doesn't sound like her Wick, but for the moment she can see the old him in his eyes. It is the look of someone pausing to take a final breath in the middle of his own drowning.

The Thunderbird has already been sold, weeks ago, to help pay the mortgage. Ruth and Gary sold it for her in Orlando. Amelia never could find a way to bring the thing back home. As for the rest of Wick's wishes, Amelia does as she is told, and they never do go back. Sometimes, at night, Amelia drives past the hospital by herself, wishing she had a grave to visit instead.

Maybe I needed to explain the story to Noel and Daniel. Retell it in a way they'd understand. We'd been driving in silence for nearly 30 minutes since I'd screamed at them. New Jersey, I was learning, was a long state. We had another day-and-a-half before we'd reach Royal, Tennessee. Even as I was thinking this, I was stuck on Claire's version, on the fact that she *had* a version. Why had she told it? Did she use it to explain something to the boys about their own dad? And was that even fair use?

The sign ahead read:

PENNSYLVANIA TURNPIKE 30 MILES
PHILADELPHIA 45 MILES

We were nearly out of the tri-state area, and soon we'd be out of the northeast altogether. I grabbed onto this fact and held it tightly. We're not on a highway, I thought, but a river, an old river to a new future.

"Dad, are you going on a trip?" said Noel. I jumped at his voice. In the mirror, Noel was waving the folded-up street map of San Francisco I'd tucked beneath the passenger seat. It was one of the places I was thinking about for when we moved on from Royal. I didn't know anyone in San Francisco, hadn't ever been there. Which made it a perfect place to disappear. If the police started asking Claire about past acquaintances, past locations, Mike and Patty might come up, but San Francisco wouldn't.

If the police start asking, I thought. There's a phrase I never thought I'd ever come to in my lifetime. I pictured myself thrown across the hood of a squad car, my children loaded into yet another backseat. I shook it off.

"That's San Francisco," I said, stupidly. "Ever been?" Noel didn't smile. This should have been the perfect opportunity to tell the boys the plan, but suddenly it wasn't. I felt caught. That might as well have been Claire back there, waving all the evidence in my face.

"So . . . you'll come back," said Noel. "Right?"

"Is there alligators in Sam Percisco?" said Daniel.

Noel was inventing a scenario in his brain, I knew, and suddenly I wanted more than anything to know where my distant, guarded son saw me going. Would he like his father better if he were further away? Did he like the idea of me getting on with my life, leaving him to start a new one with Rafe as his dad? I held Noel's gaze in the mirror, or as best I could without crashing us. "Would you want me to come back?"

Noel, as always, didn't say any of the things a parent would want his child to say. He didn't say, *Oh, my Daddy, yes! Please don't leave me!* He didn't say, *I will cry every day until you come back.* He didn't say, *Take me with you.* Instead, he bugged his eyes out at me and turned his face to the window. He was smirking. But I knew that smirk! It meant: *I'm having an emotion I don't know what to do with.* I thought: I could live for a long time on that smirk. It could get us all the way to Royal, Tennessee.

"What were the people's names?" said Daniel.

I smiled at him. I was so in love with that high little voice. It was so nice to have two boys who were so different, yet each a crucial part of their father's heart. Noel and Daniel, my negative and positive, my Yin and Yang.

"What people, sweetie?"

"The people on the plane," said Daniel.

"Hey, yeah," said Noel. "Was it an accident? Or was it like terrorists?"

"What's a tourerist?" said Daniel.

And like that, there was no floor or seat beneath me. I was hurtling down the highway strapped to the front of my own car. In all the years since I'd first heard the story from my aunt Ruth, all the times I'd told it to others, it had never occurred to me to wonder about the people on the plane. What was that like for them, in their final moments? And where were they going? For the first time, I found myself picturing the rows of passengers. Some were maybe starting new lives in Florida, some were coming back from somewhere. And some of them were just taking a vacation, happy to get away for a bit but already a little eager to go home. As the plane went down, all of them, each in his or her own way, was surely thinking, *This is not what I'd planned.*

Suddenly, the act of running away with my children was not the cathartic rush it had been just a moment ago. Instead, it was a hollow, ghostly feeling, as if I were somewhere in the sky above, watching the three of us go. From up there, the car looked like a toy, my big idea for saving us all like a random nothing, a fluff of milkweed floating on the wind.

"What was grandma like when she was younger?" said Daniel. "Is the accident how her smile got broke?"

And that was all I could take. I hit the turn signal, took my foot off the gas, and let them drift toward the service area that'd popped up on the right, seemingly without notice, out of either reprieve or mockery. The I Knew You Couldn't Do It! Service Area.

"Why are we going this way?" said Noel. He looked around. "Where even are we?" I said nothing. Daniel leaned against his brother as they rode the long, tight curve of the exit ramp, their new river to the old future.

"Now are we getting corn?" said Daniel.

* * *

Two years after the crash, a man asks for Amelia's hand. He is a tax accoun-
tant with the means to take care of Amelia and her young son—not in wealth,
but in modest style, which to them at this point sure looks a lot like wealth.
Amelia doesn't wait for another opportunity; she can't afford to. She will not
love Joseph Barney, she will not really know him. At holidays, there will be
embarrassing moments where Amelia has baked treats with nutmeg, to which
Joseph is mildly allergic. It was Wick who'd loved nutmeg. But she has kept
her promise to Wick: She and her son are taken care of. And the troubled, still-
restless boy grows up knowing an organized, careful man as his father, with
no idea of how he could have come from this person.

Ten minutes later, we were back on the Turnpike and heading north
again. The kids sipped at the giant sodas I'd bought them inside the
service area, and I could hear the last of their peanut M&M's rolling
around on the floor, clacking into each other between the huge pairs
of feet.

I had now been made to promise to bring back a Giants hat for
Noel when I returned from my mythical trip to San Francisco. Though,
in fact, it may not have been a bad idea to go somewhere new, just for
a visit, to prove I could travel beyond the 300-mile rut I'd dug between
New Hampshire and New York. Daniel wanted me to bring back a
Spider-Man toy. I opened my mouth to explain to Daniel that you
could get a Spider-Man from anywhere, and wouldn't he rather have
something you could only find in San Francisco, but I stopped myself
and instead shared a grin in the mirror with Noel, both of us thinking,
Oh, Daniel. This was as good as it may ever get between Noel and me,
I knew. I'd take it.

My children, unbeknownst to themselves, had foiled a nefarious
plot. And while Damaged Loser wasn't as good as World's Greatest
Dad, it still might be preferable to Kidnapper/"Area Man"/Prisoner
Number Such-and-Such. And I wasn't Rafe, true, but then perhaps *Rafe*
wouldn't be Rafe—that is, the man my wife wanted—if it hadn't been
for me.

Maybe, when they're grown, I will tell my boys what their father
nearly did that one weird Sunday after the long visitation. And I hope
they'll see not a cracked jackass but a man driven to extremes by love.
Just as that boy born in Orlando in 1966 would later learn that his

father—his real father—was the kind of man who would use his body to shield his wife and unborn child from a plummeting airplane. As if that could possibly have been enough, as if that alone could have preserved the lives beneath him.

Guests of Honor

Back in high school, Night-Swarm used to say his disguise made his head a smooth black dome, terrifying in its inscrutability. The "disguise" was a scuba hood worn over a dirt-bike mask. Both were made of stretchy black neoprene. I wouldn't let him wear the gear when we were hanging out, but I knew he wore it when he was alone. Now, six years after graduation, Night-Swarm had put on weight and grown his hair, and the gear made his head more like a black potato, disturbing in its lumpiness. He couldn't find the old cape, I guess, but that didn't stop the former Kevin Wakefield from showing up at my mother's house on a hot July night in 2006, wearing the ridiculous hood-mask combo, along with his black nylon jacket from the Watch It! Security Company.

We'd found the jacket together at the St. Vincent De Paul thrift store. The patch on the front had said *ALLEN*. Kevin had liked that—a good, forgettable identity, he said—so he kept the patch. Not long after he'd bought it, someone sneaked into his locker, took a Sharpie to the second "L," and made it into *ALIEN*. I was pissed. Kevin didn't mind the vandalism so much as he minded everyone calling him Alien instead of Night-Swarm.

We hadn't hung out much in the six years since high school. I mean, I was no social tornado myself, and I'd long since come to the conclusion that Night-Swarm was just sandbags around my ankles. But here he was, at my mother's door on a Friday evening, asking for one last hang-out before he went away. He wouldn't tell me where he was going, saying I'd find out in a bit. *"Please,* Pat," he'd said, and I think that's what did it—if he'd called me Panic Boy, his old high-school name for me, I'd have shut the door in his face.

"I got a bangin' party in Worcester," I told him. "I'll hang with you a bit. Hour, tops." The party wasn't a lie: I just didn't know where it was yet. I was waiting for the call from my boy Trevor.

I'd spent the last year converting my wardrobe, evolving from non-skating skater-guy to hip-hop, under the influence of Trevor and my other coworkers at New England Carpet. I was the only white employee, hence their nickname for me: Guest of Honor. When Night-Swarm showed up that evening, I was dressed for my night out: Roc-a-Wear jeans, Adidas track jacket, everything low and loose. I was careful not to go too crazy with it: No gold, for instance—there are just some things a twenty-four-year-old white boy can't get away with—but at least I looked more *XXL* than *Mother Jones.*

Neither of us had a car at the moment, so we walked downtown. I refused to go unless he took off the hood and left it at my mother's house, so Night-Swarm's sweaty face shone and glistened in the streetlamps like a ham in a can. His Watch It! jacket swished as he walked.

The only things open past 8:00 on Main Street in our town were the Hog's Head Tavern, a pair of pizza places, and the Italian restaurant that kept changing its name, as if that was the problem. Night-Swarm steered us toward the Hog's Head.

Two girls from our class, Jen and Andrea, were standing a few feet up from the door of the bar, smoking cigarettes and staring at our approach. I'd always had a thing for both of them in high school: Metal-shop girls wore the tightest jeans and the biggest hair. They were still pretty now, in a waitressy way, blonde and hard-mouthed. They stood, as ever, under a cloud of menthol smoke.

"Evening, ladies," said Night-Swarm. "All good in the hood?" He turned to me and winked.

The sight of them brought me right back to high school, when my role had been co-freak to Night-Swarm. I had to remind myself that we were finally past that shit now. We were twenty-four, not sixteen. They were women and I was a man. And a far different person than the one they'd known.

"Hey, faggots," said Andrea.

"Holy shit, Pat and Alien?" said Jen, "I haven't seen you guys in forever." (*Fa-revah,* she really said, in her Central Massachusetts accent, which to me was still like a rusty nail being pulled from a board.)

"Please," said Night-Swarm. "Call me Night-Swarm. For one last night, anyway."

What *was* all this one-last-night business? I wanted to ask him, but I suddenly didn't want the girls to know I'd pretty much abandoned Night-Swarm. They'd known him since kindergarten, and had always been a little protective of him.

"Yeah, okay," said Jen. "Night-Swarm it is."

He smiled. "So can I buy you ladies a drink?" said Night-Swarm. "Panic Man?"

I ignored the name and pulled out my cell. No voice mail, no texts. I set it to vibrate. I needed only to know where the party was happening. At first buzz, I'd be gone.

"Lead the way," I said, and followed Night-Swarm and the girls into the bar.

Credit where credit's due: It was Night-Swarm who'd once talked me out of getting violent in school. It was sophomore year and my mother and I had just moved to Massachusetts from Portland, Maine. The Hillsville kids, geniuses that they were, immediately named me Pepperidge Farm. I was made fun of for reading books that weren't assigned, got punched between my shoulder blades for having an earring, was told my divorced mother was a hairy dyke.

So I was in the cafeteria making a list of names (this was a year before Columbine, so no judgments) when I looked up and saw a chubby guy standing in line, wearing a black cape. People yelled and hooted and laughed, but the guy just stood there, whapping his empty tray against his stomach, like a little kid might. As far as he was concerned, he was just waiting for his lasagna. I wondered who would choose that kind of torture for themselves. I also thought he looked like the kind of guy who might be interested in taking some revenge. When he came off the lunch line, I waved him over.

But Kevin Wakefield turned out not to be the revenge type. "None of this is permanent, you know," he said.

"Yeah, but wouldn't you like to wipe out some of those snotty looks?" I said.

"My mom says it's because they don't like themselves," he said.

"Then they should kill themselves."

Wakefield pointed his fork at me. "My friend, I think you're suffering from something called a hardening of the attitudes."

"Your mom tell you that, too?"

He shook his head. "Loretta LaRoche."

"The PBS lady?" Apparently we had similar household viewing habits.

"Anyway," said Kevin Wakefield. "I'm looking for someone who shares my interest in fighting for truth and justice. Is that you?"

"I don't care. I'm just trying to get through the day without being spit on."

"Think it over," he said. "And think of a good name for yourself. Mine's Night-Swarm, so don't take that one. You should pick something unique and menacing, but not too flashy."

"Sure. Got it." I wasn't really going to think of some hero name, but it was good having someone to sit with. Later, Night-Swarm would decide my name should be Panic Man. I never answered to it, but he never stopped saying it, either. All the same, I'd be lying if I said it wasn't nice to have someone to hang around and read comics with, talk a little harmless crazy-talk. We'd never do any of the things Night-Swarm claimed to want to do, the whole cleaning-up-the-world business, and that was fine with me.

"And don't you dare skip that brownie," said Night-Swarm, pointing to my plate. "It's the best thing they make here."

A small Massachusetts town like Hillsville would never have just one bar—in fact, we had twelve, mostly on the outskirts—but the Hog's Head was the only one you could access with a learner's permit. The owner was a six-and-a-half-foot tall skinhead named Finger. Finger was called that because he was minus the ring finger on his left hand. Every year, he held something called HogFest on his parents' farm, which was out on the edge of town. Night-Swarm and I had never gone to HogFest, of course, but like everyone else, we heard the stories about all-day-music, free pot, and freaky sex. The cops were too scared of Finger to bust him. I could understand. My first day of school, lost in the hallways, I turned a corner and found Finger standing over the crumpled, wheezing body of the principal I'd met just an hour earlier. Finger still had his fists at his sides, like a pair of knobby hammers.

He looked up at me and grinned. "You got a hall pass?" he said, as if he'd been waiting for someone to come along just so he could say his line. The principal recovered, but Finger had made his impression on both of us.

The bar at the Hog's Head was in the center of the room, a square of oak with a pit in the middle. Here Finger stalked and bobbed like a point guard for the Aryan Nation All-Stars. As we walked in, dozens of goatees and baseball hats turned toward us. A group of girls in acid-wash miniskirts circa 19-fucking-90 pointed and laughed. Not at Night-Swarm, at *me*. Someone said *wigger*.

I leaned in to Night-Swarm: "A wretched hive of scum and villainy."

He elbowed me in the chest. Night-Swarm always hated when I dropped *Star Wars* quotes. To him, things like *Star Wars* and *Dungeons & Dragons* were dumb because they were impossible. Superheroes, said Night-Swarm, were not impossible, just unproven.

"Alien, can I buy you a Sprite?" said Andrea. She had her hand on his arm.

"It's Night-Swarm," he said gently. "And no thank you, Andrea. I have some business to attend to." Then he turned and headed for the bar.

Night-Swarm got Finger's attention, then reached into his security-guard jacket. For a second, I thought he was going to shiv Finger, deliver some actual justice before going wherever he was going. Was this what he'd spent the last years working up to? He'd always talked about cleaning up Hillsville, and Finger was the natural (possibly only) choice. But when Night-Swarm's hand reappeared, it was holding a ball of paper.

Finger leaned in, and they whispered to each other. Then Finger stood up, holding the ball. He cupped his hands: "Yo, listen up! Night-Swan here—"

"*Swarm,*" yelled Night-Swarm.

"—has just bought drinks for everyone. Motherfucker's shipping off to Iraq or whatever tomorrow, so come up and say goodbye while he's still got a face." He pointed to Night-Swarm, who grinned at the crowd. "Night-Swan, everybody!"

I couldn't feel my legs, only two tingly tubes that were holding me up somehow. Iraq? He was going to Iraq? And he couldn't have told me before the rest of these fucking people?

Meanwhile, everyone rushed that bar like it was made of drugs.

* * *

When I'd started in the warehouse at New England Carpet, the other guys there, mostly African Americans and Haitian immigrants, looked at me as an adorable curiosity, and I was adopted. Panic Man was dead; long live Guest of Honor. I'd spent all high school trying to get laid, in spite of myself, in spite of Night-Swarm, with nothing to show for it. My first few years after high school weren't any better. It was like I had a stink on me that I couldn't shake. Then, a week after starting at the warehouse, I went to one of Trevor's parties and ended up losing my cherry to a thirty-two-year-old community-college teacher. I was finally with the right people.

Trevor told me later he liked to import his female party guests. He had friends all over, and his parties were good enough that these guys would bring as many girls ("Talent," Trevor called them) as possible. The idea being that a local girl, if she didn't like the vibe, would just walk right out, whereas a visitor would be more likely to settle for whatever situation she'd traveled to get to.

And this was what was going on right now, somewhere maybe twelve miles away, without me. All day, I'd been picturing the crew from work—Trevor, Donald, Benny, *me*—drinking good scotch, getting all grinded up on by some asstastic girls from Fall River or Providence.

Then Night-Swarm had come along and fucked me up with this going-to-war business. All I could picture now was Kevin Wakefield in his cape, standing in the middle of some hot, yellow Mars halfway around the world, whapping his Marine-issue lunch tray against his stomach.

It took seven minutes for the Hog's Head to drink up all of Night-Swarm's cash. People came back for seconds and thirds, and no one said *Thank You.* People did say *Good Luck*—or, more accurately, *Good fucking luck, dude,* which is not the same thing. When the money ran out, people went right back to ignoring Night-Swarm.

"Panic Man," he said. "Do you have any money on you?"

"Shipping out?" I said. "Iraq? You couldn't have told me these things at my house? On our way down?"

He smiled at me, his eyes so calm and clear I had to look away first. "I heard the call," he said. "Someone has to defend our freedoms."

He took a sloppy set of papers from inside his jacket and unfolded them for me. According to the United States Marine Corps, he was now Private Kevin Sharpe Wakefield, pay grade E-1.

"Please, Pat," he said. "Money? Any?"

In my pocket I had three hundred dollars. It was my going-out money, my contribution to Trevor's booze-and-whatever-else fund, not good for legal tender in cow-town. I put my hand around it. Then I thought of Night-Swarm's little betrayal tonight. "I got, like, seven dollars," I told him.

"Well, crap," he said. "What am I gonna do?"

"You owe Finger more?"

"No, but I spent what I had, and people were just beginning to enjoy themselves. That was all the money I got for selling my car."

I wasn't sure I'd heard this right. "You sold your car. To buy drinks for the worst people in Hillsville."

He smiled, like I was the stupid one. "These are all the people I know."

A little guy from the class ahead of ours came over. I couldn't remember his name; he was four-foot-something, so everyone had always just called him Tree. "Yo, man," said Tree, pointing up at Night-Swarm. "You're my fucking *hero,* man."

"Well, thank you," said Night-Swarm. "Did you have some drinks?"

"Yeah, so the time you got caught jerking off alone in the auditorium? That was hard-core."

"Ah," said Night-Swarm. His face darkened, but he never stopped smiling. I'd heard about the auditorium thing when I first got to Hillsville. What had made the impression on me wasn't the story so much as what everyone said he did the next day. What he did was, he came back to school. Most people wouldn't have come back at all.

"You still at the Stop & Shop?" said Tree.

Night-Swarm nodded. "Assistant Store Manager."

"Really?" I said. Last time I'd seen Night-Swarm, he was working the counter at a Blockbuster.

"So I'm shipping out Sunday," Night-Swarm told Tree, "Parris Island. Then I go and fight for freedom and democracy. I'll probably end up with an M40A3, that's a sniper rifle. Bomb-proof, solid as a rock at eight hundred yards."

I looked at him. He'd always hated guns. Said they were against his code.

"All right," Tree nodded. "My cousin was over there."

"Really? And he's back now?"

"Naw. Buncha guys came up at a stoplight and pulled him off the back of his Humvee. Broad daylight, cut off his head. Then the crowd—just regular people—they rushed in and *kicked* his body to mush. You believe that?"

Night-Swarm said nothing. For the first time all night, his smile was gone. It was a sight more terrifying than my image of him in the desert.

I stepped between them. "Go away, Tree."

"What? It happened."

"Get the fuck out," I said.

"Cool, I gotta take a piss anyways," said Tree. "You nail one of those raggers for me, will ya? For my cousin?"

"Yeah," said Night-Swarm. Even in the dark, his face looked gray.

"Oh, hey," said Tree. "So I guess that Stop & Shop job's open now?"

I stepped toward him, and he scurried away.

"You okay?" I said to Night-Swarm. "Want me to walk you home?"

Night-Swarm shook his head, but he still wasn't smiling.

I took him out to the sidewalk. "Can you get out of it?" I said.

He stared at me. "Not an option, Pat."

"Why? You could cut a finger off or something."

"I have a commitment and a purpose," he said. "Have you still never believed in anything?"

I didn't answer. I believed in weed and pussy, but I wasn't going to tell him that. After a while, I had an idea. It made my stomach churn, but I couldn't look at him like this anymore, all quiet and freaked-out. "You never had a theme song," I said.

"What?" Night-Swarm looked tired, suddenly, vaguely irritated.

"Okay, listen," I said. I'd never rapped for anyone before. There are certain boundaries that, as a white person, you just don't cross. For Night-Swarm, though, I took a breath and began to freestyle.

Night-Swarm, Night-Swarm
Comin' down like a
Fright storm
Deviating from the
White norm
Bringing wrong niggas some
Right harm
Shovelin' killers to the
Max dorm
Night-Swarm, Night-Swarm
Night-Swarm, Night-Swarm

When I was done, I cleared my throat. "What did you think?" I asked him, not looking him in the eye.

"I'm chuffed," said Night-Swarm. I looked up to see what this could possibly mean. He was grinning, so I guessed *chuffed* was good. "What's a 'max dorm'?" he said.

"Maximum security prison," I said.

"See, I wouldn't have known that. I guess you're really up on your street lingo."

The heat went on in my face. "I made it up. Needed an 'orm' rhyme to get back on track from 'harm.'"

"That's a lot to have to think of as you go. I never realized."

"End rhyme can be a bitch, yo."

We walked back inside, me holding the door open for him. As he ducked under my outstretched arm, I could hear him chanting: *Night-Swarm, Night-Swarm. . . .* I hung back just a second, letting myself linger on the satisfaction of having done my part. This body was guilt-free. I checked my phone again and then went inside.

Fast-forward to 2:00. Closing time in Ye Olde Commonwealth. Some musty Guns N' Roses song on the jukebox, the endless fucker that starts out as a ballad, then gets really fast and loud and screechy. People slow danced, even through the fast part, just like we used to do in high school for "Free Bird" and "Dream On." Love songs for the red-necked and drunk. Massachusetts is full of factory towns that haven't produced anything in decades. In Hillsville, I'm certain, they stopped manufacturing memories in the 80s. Night-Swarm was dancing with shop-class Andrea. She was sloppy-drunk, and he was dragging her around in messy circles. I was a little shit-faced myself. I'd left two messages for Trevor in Worcester, hoping I didn't sound like a little bitch waiting on her prom date.

I'd also been drinking and talking with Andrea's buddy Jen for the last hour. Jen was a welder now. She'd just spent the week working down inside one of those huge, white water tanks you see sometimes when you're driving along the highway. This was a brand-new one, and Jen was inside it, welding the seams.

"When you're down in those things, with no top on them," said Jen, "it's like being in a crater on the moon. All you can see is sky, nothing else. You feel so tiny. Invisible." She shivered. "It got me started thinking about what if our entire world is like a single hair on the back of this microscopic whatever that's in a dish on some alien lab guy's table?

And, like, when's he going to get around to just tossing us out?" We
looked at each other for a long moment, longer than you're supposed
to. There was a good chance I wasn't getting to that party tonight. Also,
I couldn't stop picturing Jen naked, wearing only her welder's mask. I
had a sudden notion to salvage things where I could.

I leaned in to Jen. Trevor had a line he used with a lot of success,
and it seemed like exactly the thing to say at that moment. "Baby, if
you let me go down on you," I whispered. "I will make you feel like the
most important person on earth."

Jen's eyebrow went up, but nothing else changed on her face. She
leaned in, and her nose brushed my cheek. Something twitched in my
pants. "My ride's leaving soon," she whispered. I watched her walk to
the bar, where Finger leaned across the counter and kissed her with a
big, open mouth. Then she whispered something to him. He looked
over at me and gave the thumbs-up and a smirk that chilled my gut.

Night-Swarm and Andrea appeared beside me. He was leaning into
her, and she was very much leaning away from him. "Panic Man!" said
Night-Swarm. "There's a whole coterie heading over to Finger's for an
after-hours gathering. We are to be his special guests."

"Sounds bangin'," I said. "I think I need to go the fuck home."

"Oh, come now," said Night-Swarm. "Please?" He used his eyes to
motion toward Andrea.

Andrea caught his look. She turned to me. "Yeah, but Pat looks
like he needs some help getting home," said Andrea. She glared. "You
need help, right, Pat?"

I was drunker than I'd thought, and I caught on too late. Night-
Swarm threw his arm around Andrea and me. "Splendid! We're all
going to Finger's!"

We rode in the back of Andrea's pickup truck. She drove fast, and
seemed to enjoy taking the corners so that we slid around the truck
bed like duffel bags. Somewhere, in between all the hard turns, my
phone buzzed.

"You looking for me?" said a voice. Trevor!

"Aww, shit!" I said. I could hear party noise in the background.
Sweet, sweaty freedom. It was like someone had thrown open a big,
sunny window in the middle of all this darkness. "It's Guest of Honor,"
I said. "Where you fellas at?" Night-Swarm was looking at me now. I put
my head down so I could get some privacy.

"You missing big tonight, son. Benny's place, three kegs, talent aplenty. Got some girls from Providence, Hartford. Couple locals, too. Young Verne's in the back bedroom with that girl from payroll you like. What's her name?"

"Yvonne?" I said. I'd wanted Yvonne for months. Yvonne never came to parties. It couldn't be Yvonne.

"That's the one. She was all over my shit earlier, but I passed her to Young Verne."

"Damn."

Night-Swarm tapped my leg. He mouthed, "Everything okay?" I waved him off.

"All right," said Trevor. "Well, it's gonna roll on till morning. We'll fill you in on Monday, I guess. You missing out, Wiggy Boy."

There was a pause, clinking glasses in one ear and wind in the other as I tried to figure out what I'd just heard. "What did you call me?" I said.

Trevor laughed into the phone. "Aw, shit," he said. "Did I just say it?" In the background I heard someone yell, "Who's on the phone? Is that Wiggy? Wiggy Boy, you *adorable,* baby. Keep on—" and the line went dead.

I snapped the phone closed.

"Everything all right?" said Night-Swarm.

"Just shut up," I said. Then I turned and wedged myself into the corner of the truck bed, so I wouldn't have to look at him.

We finally came to a little metal bridge that rattled like a box of empty cans when we crossed it, and then we were on a winding dirt road. I didn't see or hear any animals at Finger's farm, but there was a huge, gleaming greenhouse that was three times the size of the ranch house that sat on the other side of the gravel driveway. In between these two buildings was a big red barn with a huge pumpkin logo on the front. When four other cars pulled up and it seemed like everyone was there who would be there, Finger led us all toward the barn. I watched him, waiting to be stabbed for offering to eat out his girlfriend. *Wiggy Boy,* I thought. At that moment I'd have welcomed a stabbing. As we walked in, I glanced over at the greenhouse. It was lit in that low-wattage greenhouse style, the color of too-early morning, the color of headaches. There was a pot leaf stenciled on the door. In the middle of the leaf was a white swastika.

Finger saw me looking, and grinned. "Keeps away the curious."

"Gotta protect those pumpkins," I said.

"Right," he laughed. "The pumpkins *always* need protecting." The way he said it, he might have been saying, "The heads *always* need cutting off."

Inside, the barn was nicer than my mom's house. There was a wood-plank floor, not a scrap of hay in sight, the lighting golden and warm. At the near wall, by the entrance, was a small bar, stocked with tall bottles, miles better than what he offered at the Hog's Head. A few feet in front of that was a brown leather couch that could easily seat six. And at the back wall, taped up between an armoire and an old green refrigerator, was the paper silhouette of a man. It was filled with holes.

There were about a dozen of us in the barn. It was about three-to-one, males to females, but I was grateful for the girls we had; they kept it from feeling too prison-y. I wiped my forehead, wishing I'd had both less and more to drink. Over by the bar, Finger took off his shirt. His huge chest and arms were filthy with tattoos, including a nasty-looking eagle and a couple of iron crosses.

"Who's first?" he said. What, I thought: First to get beat up? First to do Russian roulette?

I realized I was the only one still near the door. Not wanting to be volunteered for whatever this was, I skanked over to where Night-Swarm had planted himself by Andrea. I phrased my question in the form of a DMX lyric: "What type of games is bein' played / How's it goin' down?" I tried to do it like DMX, but it came out shaky and nasally, so *white. Wiggy Boy, you adorable!*

Andrea leaned in and put her mouth against my ear. "Don't know, don't care. If you get Alien away from me, I'll promise you a handjob."

Before I could answer, Finger said, "Fuck it, then. I'll go first." Then he reached behind the bar and pulled out a long, skinny canvas bag, wider at one end than the other. He unzipped it and let the bag drop to the floor. What was left in his hands was a military-looking rifle with a big scope on its barrel.

"Ruger thirty-aught-six," said Night-Swarm. "Nice piece, Finger."

Finger tipped the gun toward Night-Swarm. "Check out the eye on Night-Horn. Impressive."

I looked over at Night-Swarm. He had his arms folded across his chest and was smiling, like this was his element. Like he'd suddenly dropped into a groove he'd somehow missed during every other moment in his life. Or like everyone else had finally caught up with him. I moved over next to him. In his big, sweaty ear, I whispered the truth. That everyone in the room thought he was ridiculous, that they'd invited him here as a joke, knowing he wouldn't have the good sense to say no. That the night would probably end with him getting beat to shit, just for someone else's fun. When I was done, he didn't move, didn't speak. I saw his jaw bulge a little at the hinge, but that was it.

Finger knelt behind the couch and propped the rifle across the back of it. Half a breath ago, there'd been people sitting on that couch, but they'd all cleared out and were standing with the rest of us.

"Take it, bitch," whispered Finger. There was a huge sound, and a fresh blister popped on the paper torso of the silhouette.

"Fuck yeah!" yelled the guys.

"Go Finger!" yelled Andrea.

"You're so awesome, honey," said Jen. She leaned down and kissed his bald head.

Finger moved back to the bar. Another guy, some shaggy dude in his thirties, went next. He hit the edge of the silhouette man, just outside the elbow. His girlfriend applauded. A few people made "Woo!" noises, but we all could see he was no Finger.

Finger took back the rifle and turned toward me. "Yo, Eminem. Have a go?" He offered the Ruger.

It was so much heavier than I'd imagined it would be. It felt solid and perfect, even the wood, like there was nothing on Earth that could dent it or scratch it. If I'd had one of these in high school, I thought, I wouldn't have to be here now. Then I pictured Finger sitting inside his greenhouse, giggling like a baby as he lined up the door in his crosshairs and waited for the DEA to finish landing their faggot-ass helicopters on his sovereign soil.

I'd never shot a gun before, so I tried to do everything like Finger had. I knelt behind the couch and held the gun against my shoulder. I knew you were supposed to hold the thing as tightly as possible, to keep it from kicking back at you.

I sighted the paper guy in the scope. "Make a kill shot," said Finger, "and I'll let you do what you said to Jennifer." Much laughter, A-ha-ha. I didn't hear Jen's voice in there.

I pretended the guy on the wall was Finger. I'll admit, I even thought of Trevor and Young Verne. Had they really been calling me one thing to my face and another behind my back all this time?

I pulled the trigger and my right ear went dead. I never heard the bullet hit. My shoulder felt like it'd been kicked by a horse. My stomach did, too, and then something in me twisted and churned until I could feel it lurching at the back of my throat. I got up and handed the gun to Finger.

"Gotta piss," I said, trying to sound as careless as possible.

"Hope you don't piss like you shoot," Finger called after me. "You just hit my fridge."

I made it to the grass between the house and the barn, then brought up breakfast, lunch, and dinner. Every time I stood up to go inside, my stomach hauled me back down to my knees. After every heave, I slapped myself in the face for being a pussy and a lightweight. Finally, I seemed to be done. I got to my feet, then walked over and pissed all over Finger's greenhouse door, soaking the knob.

Back in the barn, Night-Swarm was kneeling at the couch, the rifle tight against his shoulder. I stood behind Finger and Jen.

"Man of the hour," Finger said. "God and country." He looked around, grinning.

"Semper Fi, you Alien motherfucker!" Jen yelled.

"Come on, big boy," someone said. "Show us what you're gonna do to the sand niggers."

There was a moment of peace, then, an instant where no one was shouting or snickering, and I saw Night-Swarm's jaw bulge again. And then I felt it: He was going to wheel around and start firing. I'd planted the bug in his ear, popped his little bubble, and now he was going to take everyone out, me included.

But Night-Swarm just stretched his neck, cleared his throat, and adjusted the stock in the hollow of his shoulder. He took in a deep breath to steady the shot—something I realized I'd forgotten to do—then leaned forward and pulled the trigger.

His head flipped back. A spray of blood arced through the air behind him, toward us. Finger screamed something about backfire, blocked chambers. Andrea just screamed. I tasted salty metal in my mouth. When I wiped my hand against my tongue, it came back red.

Night-Swarm was on the floor. Finger and I knelt at opposite shoulders. Night-Swarm's right eyebrow was gone. In its place was a flapping wound. Blood spread across his forehead and into his eye, or where his eye was supposed to be. It was hard to tell. He was silent and still. I thought: *You stupid motherfucker. Even God knows you don't belong in a war.*

Finger yelled, "Towel! Give me a towel!" Someone threw him the shirt he'd taken off. He hesitated a second, then pressed it to Night-Swarm's head.

"Dude, can you talk?" said Finger. He was as pale as Night-Swarm. "Oh my fucking god, please say something."

"Ugga bine," said Night-Swarm.

"Oh, man, that's not even English," wailed Finger. "That's not good, is it?"

Andrea was still screaming. I heard scuffling, then the barn door. A moment later, a bunch of cars peeled away. No one wanted to be an accessory.

Night-Swarm looked more alert than I'd have thought. He wasn't crying, he wasn't moaning. He was just moving that one bare eye back and forth between Finger and me. Was this what death looked like?

But Finger saw something different. "Wait a minute," he said. He took Night-Swarm's hand and pressed it against the shirt on his forehead. Then Finger leaned over and picked up the rifle. He turned it over in his hands.

"Dude?" he said to Night-Swarm. He held the rifle over him so he could see it with his good eye. A drop of blood fell from the eyepiece of the scope and landed on Night-Swarm's nose.

"Stupid, you didn't *shoot* yourself," said Finger. "You fucking *gouged* yourself with the scope."

"Oh my god," said Jen. "Haven't you ever shot a rifle before?"

"I know what I'm doing," said Night-Swarm. He sat up, looking confused, like an old man in a big parking lot.

"Christ," said Finger. He jerked his shirt away from Night-Swarm, then went behind the bar and poured a shot for himself.

"I know what I'm doing!" yelled Night-Swarm again.

I reached down and put a hand on his shoulder, but he swatted it away.

His eye was okay, but the bleeding wouldn't stop, so Andrea said she'd take Night-Swarm to the hospital in Worcester. I volunteered to ride along; I wasn't thinking anymore about my party, or about the handjob I'd been promised.

I bumped along in the back of Andrea's truck, sitting on the wheel-well. Night-Swarm rode up front with Andrea. I'd given him my Adidas zip-up for him to hold against his cut. He'd wanted to use his Watch It! Security Company jacket, but I wouldn't let him ruin it more than it already was. He'd already lost his dignity, and nearly his eye.

Through the little cab window, I could watch Andrea and Night-Swarm. Their hands were clasped together on the seat between them. It didn't look romantic; it was more like little kids, how one will reach for the other if something scary's going on. I sat in the back of the speeding truck, huddled like a stowaway, freezing my ass off. At one point, not far from the center of our town, I felt a buzzing against my leg, but I didn't reach for the phone. Whatever hilarity my good friends from the warehouse had snickered up in the last hour, they could leave it on my voice mail. All I wanted to do now was help get Night-Swarm whatever help he needed. He was, all along, the only real friend I'd ever had.

The truck slowed, and I looked around. There was one stoplight in Hillsville, Massachusetts, at the top of the rise just past the Hog's Head, and we were at it. Andrea slid open the cab window and said, "Okay, you can jump out now."

"But we're not there yet."

"*You* are," she said. "Hurry up, before the light turns green."

"But—"

"Go ahead, Pat," said Night-Swarm.

I got up and hauled myself over the side of her truck. I stood there in the street, looking at them sitting inside the cozy little cab. It was a long, awkward moment while the light stayed red, but I didn't know what else to do. I couldn't imagine what else to do. Then Night-Swarm rolled down his window and said, in his high, soft voice, "Go home, Pat. You're free of me now. Wish me luck, okay?" Then the light turned green and they were gone, a pair of taillights growing tinier in the dark.

I never went back to New England Carpet, never saw Trevor and the guys again. Instead, I slept for a week at my mother's house, then borrowed money from her so I could go start my new life, or at least restart life in a new place. Those are not the same things, of course. I picked my location by spinning a globe and stopping it with my finger. It could've been anywhere; I could be in Mumbai right now, or Saigon. Where I landed seems appropriate, though.

Los Angeles isn't an easy town to make friends in, but I'm not trying all that hard, either. If no one knows you, no one can mock you. I have a set of dishes and a futon from the Salvation Army, and I have a driving job at a car-rental company. Seven days a week I escort travelers—vacationers, business people—from the fancy hotels on La Cienega or Sunset to their various terminals at LAX airport. I know one route in Los Angeles, really, really well, and I can tell you which departure terminal to use for any of the ninety-one airlines that will fly you away from here. On the phone, my mother tells me I must be in paradise, with the weather and the girls and whatnot. I always say, Yes, I sure must be. She never asks me what I'm planning for my life, just as I never tell her I'm seeing her notion of paradise through a four-foot rectangle of windshield. And for the time being, maybe that's all I should be allowed.

My neighborhood is run-down and scary, and there are gunshots every night, yet there's also a palm tree that looms right outside my apartment window. That's Los Angeles for you. I got a letter from Mrs. Wakefield a few months back—Kevin's mother. I know I should open it, that she might be passing along greetings from her son, or just wishing me well. But she might not be, and so I leave it the fuck alone. Instead, I prefer to imagine Kevin Wakefield out in his vast desert, pausing under a tree just like the one outside my window. His heavy automatic is slung over his shoulder as he scans the distance through a futuristic-looking set of binoculars. He sights a Toyota pickup gathering speed in the distance. A funnel of dust billows from the rear of the truck as it shrinks the gap between itself and a cluster of temporary buildings. He drops the binoculars and swings his weapon into position. He shoulders the stock, gets his eye against the sight—but not *right* against it—putting the Toyota in the crosshairs. And as he nestles his finger calmly against the hot metal of the trigger, getting ready to do the job he knows he was destined to do, I like to imagine him chanting to himself:

Night-Swarm, Night-Swarm
Night-Swarm, Night-Swarm

Mr. Cake-for-Breakfast

Just the LaPine men at the dinner table tonight, eleven-year-old Miles and his father, Dennis. It's the Sunday before Thanksgiving, 1981. Miles' mother is down in Florida, taking care of Grammy LaPine, who's had a small stroke. Grammy LaPine is Dennis' mother; she and her son haven't spoken in a while. Meanwhile, Carrie, Miles' fifteen-year-old sister, is AWOL again, though their dad has yet to seem concerned.

Miles' mother calls her husband Mr. Cake-for-Breakfast, the implication being that he can't be trusted to keep everyone properly fed. So far this is technically untrue, at least where breakfast is concerned. He's been leaving for work well before Miles comes down in the morning. Twice this week, Miles has awakened only five minutes before the bus arrives. Breakfast, cakey or otherwise, has not been an issue. Dinner is another story. Right now Miles is killing off his third bowl of Count Chocula. The spoon shakes in his hand, his eyeballs feel like skinned knees.

His father sits sidesaddle in his dining chair, squinting at Dan Rather on the living-room television. Rather's taken over the evening news only recently, and on this November night Mr. LaPine is keeping a close eye on him. A beer bottle sweats away on the bare tabletop, and a white plastic fork juts like a harpoon from an open tin of glistening sardines.

"Dad," says Miles. Nothing. "Dad." His father raises the One Minute finger. Dan Rather moves on to the next story.

Miles had stayed late after school on Friday. He'd been chosen to design the sixth grade's Holiday Wall—not a job that ever falls to the popular kids—and all weekend he's had the sickening feeling that what he'd thought was funny on Friday might not look that way on Monday. When he'd asked what the wall should look like, Ms. Hansberry just said, "Be creative." Well, there's his defense. He'd been *ordered* to be creative. Not one word about pleasant or unpleasant.

A commercial comes on. Miles can speak now. "Dad, do you think it's ever possible to be historically accurate and hilarious at the same time?"

Mr. LaPine teaches U.S. history at the high school. He turns around and squints at Miles. He does a lot of that these days, the squinting.

"Historically accurate," he says. "Well, Miles, at its core, humor is exaggeration, no? Problem is, the real thing's always much, much worse. Mostly it's genocide and disenfranchisement, over and over, sprinkled with dashes of scandal, just to keep it light. You can't possibly exaggerate it enough to make it humorous." He gives his son a flat smile, then turns back to Dan Rather. Miles goes to bed that night with a hot, worried stomach. His only hope is that Ms. Hansberry is impressed with the sophistication of his Thanksgiving effort.

Monday morning, the reaction in class is not good.

"You're a sick twist, LaPine," someone says.

"Miles, you're so queer!" shouts a girl. Copying her voice, someone else says, "Miles, you're so fat." Another girl comes in, looks at the wall, and runs out crying.

The wall is your basic scene of pilgrims, Indians, and turkeys, all fleshed in colored construction paper and detailed with brown or black magic marker. Except that all the Indians are dead, stacked like cordwood by the cabins in the background. A worried-looking turkey is stretched across a chopping stump in the foreground; over him stands a maniacal pilgrim, cradling a blood-drenched axe. The ground near the stump is littered with turkey heads. Miles would have left it all like this, but then he worried his point might be missed. So he'd added a speech bubble leading from the mouth of the doomed turkey: "Actually, guys, I hear the first Thanksgiving meal was mostly kale and seafood." Then, for one of the Indians in the body pile, he pasted in a smaller bubble that said, "Stove Top?! We're stayin'!"

"My friend," says Ms. Hansberry, "we need to talk."

At the afternoon bell, Miles heads for his locker to gather his homework. His father is there, leaning against the dented metal door. He's wearing his high-school-teacher uniform: jeans, balding corduroy jacket, and an exhausted stare. Right now he points that stare at Miles. He's never looked so tall.

They sit in Miles' homeroom, waiting for Ms. Hansberry to finish her department meeting. After a lot of shifting and sighing, Mr. LaPine gets up and stands in front of his son's desk, examining the Thanksgiving tableau on the Holiday Wall.

When Mr. LaPine turns back around, his hand is over his mouth. The face behind the hand is gathered tightly, like a sheet. He's smiling or furious, but which? Miles is about to explain everything when the door opens behind him.

Mr. LaPine crosses the room to greet Ms. Hansberry. When he introduces himself, Miles thinks for a second, "Who's 'Dennis?'" Ms. Hansberry's name, it turns out, is Joan. It doesn't really go with her; it's a name for someone taller, older.

This is Ms. Hansberry's first year teaching. She has a grape-shaped face with a wide mouth like a crescent moon, tiny nose, and huge eyes that never look uninterested. Miles pictures them open always, even when she's sleeping at night. Sometimes Miles feels like she can see him when he's at home, usually when he's doing something dumb. She's short, not much taller than some of the sixth graders, with hips the girls say are too wide for the top part of her body. She wears a lot of long skirts, too, which the girls say make her look like a walking bell. Those same girls say Miles looks like a potato. You can never win with them.

Ms. Hansberry gets down to business. "Okay, Mr. LaPine, obviously there's a—"

"Please," Mr. LaPine tells her. "Dennis." Miles looks at his father, then at Ms. Hansberry. She's blushing.

"Obviously there's a fine line I have to walk here, between artistic expression and eleven-year-old girls crying."

"Say no more," says Mr. LaPine. "As Miles may have told you, I'm at the high school. Eleventh- and twelfth-grade history."

"No, Miles has not mentioned that." Neither of them has so much as glanced at the defendant. "So you understand the position this puts me in."

"I do understand. We certainly didn't mean to put you in any sort of position."

Ms. Hansberry lets out a little breath. "So," she says. "You're up at the high school."

"Only till 3:00," says Mr. LaPine. "And then I'm not." Ms. Hansberry blushes again, and Miles turns to his father. He looks foreign, somehow, drawn wrong. Then Miles realizes: His father is smiling.

Miles is surprised to find he is not being punished. At school, yes: He has to redo the Holiday Wall. But at home there is no consequence. In fact, the next evening, Tuesday, Mr. LaPine says, cheerfully, "Let's blow this dump," and drives them out of town, toward Worcester. The muffler on the Datsun rattles and rumbles beneath them at every stoplight. After about twenty minutes, Mr. LaPine turns in at a Friendly's. "Yay!!" screams Miles. He leans across the gearshift to hug his father, but Mr. LaPine pushes him back into his seat. "Very dangerous," he says. Then he adds, "You can hug me when we park."

They pull up next to a small red car with a tattered roof of beige cloth. Mr. LaPine looks across Miles and waves. Miles turns to his right in time to see Ms. Hansberry climb up out of her little red car.

"Hey, Dad," he says. "Ms. Hansberry's here, too!"

"Now that *is* weird," says Mr. LaPine.

Inside, there's a huge, oblong lunch counter taking up most of the space, with booth tables lining the walls. A team of waitresses floats back and forth inside the counter area, yelling orders into the back room. After some protest, Ms. Hansberry agrees to join the LaPine men for dinner. Mr. LaPine requests a table by the back. The hostess scowls and says they'll have to wait a while. Mr. LaPine says this will be fine. Miles looks at his father, then at Ms. Hansberry. No one looks back at him, or at each other. To the waitresses working inside the counter area, they must look like an especially un-dangerous police lineup. Finally, Ms. Hansberry breaks the silence. "My car is a Mustang II," she tells Miles. "But I call it Son of Mustang."

"Teachers can't afford actual Mustangs, Miles," says his father. "That's why we drive a Datsun."

"It's true," says Ms. Hansberry. "Gosh, I can't even afford Cheerios. I have to buy this generic product which is all the punched-out holes swept up and snuck out of the Cheerios factory."

"Oh, Holios," says Mr. LaPine. "We used to eat those."

"We did?" says Miles.

Overhead, the grown-ups just smile at each other.

The hostess eventually parks them in a booth all the way in the back, by the bathroom hallway and kitchen entrance. The kitchen doors are made of floppy, fake wood, and they slap open and shut every time a waitress comes rushing through with a tray. Miles and his father sit across the table from Ms. Hansberry, their backs to the street-side of the restaurant. In the dim light, Ms. Hansberry's eyes look bigger than ever. She keeps them on Mr. LaPine most of the time. Except for when she glances at Miles. Then she looks away just as quickly, searching the tabletop, as if she's remembering something she was supposed to do.

Miles learns a lot during dinner at Friendly's. For one thing, Ms. Hansberry received her master's degree last year. But before that, she was in the Peace Corps for two years, teaching kids in Africa. When Mr. LaPine guesses that makes her twenty-seven, she tells him he's right. He takes her pickle. "My prize," he says.

Then there's The Delacourts. Apparently this was a band in 1966. Apparently Miles' father was in it.

"We didn't do much," says Mr. LaPine. "Gigged around." He leans back in his seat and puts an elbow up on the neck of the booth. "In Boston."

Ms. Hansberry looks impressed. Miles wants to say, "Jeez, really, Dad?" but there's now a new feeling at the table. This is not Dad but someone named Dennis, who's having dinner with a Joan. And what does that make Miles? Once, the summer he was nine, he walked to the Dairy Queen by himself. It was a big deal, and his mother had given him a dollar to buy whatever he could with it. By the time he got to the DQ, the dollar was soaked from his nervous fist. Inside he ordered, got his cone, and then stopped: There, to the right of the counter, was a table full of elementary-school teachers, ladies in shorts and t-shirts. His old third-grade teacher saw Miles staring. "Well, what did you think?" she said. "We eat ice cream, too." This is kind of like that, except he lives with one of these people.

At Friendly's, Joan says to Dennis, "My turn to guess something. Let me see, in that band you played. . . ." She stops and does her down-the-nose teacher-face at him. Then she takes up a french fry. She bites it so that they can see her large white teeth sinking into the fry. Watching this, Miles feels his legs go all sweaty. He might love her. Finally, she leans forward again and says to Dennis, "Was it . . . *guitar*?"

Dennis looks like he's thinking it over. "Bass," he says. Then he hovers his plate over hers and tilts it. "But that's a kind of guitar." His pickle rolls down into her nest of fries.

Miles watches Joan's hand as it reaches out to pick up her prize. Then it stops, frozen just above her plate. Miles looks up and into the eyes of his teacher. Ms. Hansberry is staring at him, her mouth still open, looking paler than he's ever seen her. Miles puts a hand to his own face, to wipe away whatever could be so horrifying. Already, though, Ms. Hansberry is rising from her seat. She doesn't look at either of her dinner companions. Instead, she fumbles a five-dollar bill onto the table, whispers an apology, and leaves the LaPine men sitting alone in the booth. Miles watches her hustle out of the restaurant. Mr. LaPine continues eating his fries. After a moment, he takes his pickle back from Ms. Hansberry's plate.

"I guess she had somewhere to be," says Mr. LaPine. To Miles, his voice sounds strangled and small, as if he needs a drink of water. Miles' chest swells with the sudden need to make a noise, any noise.

"So, Dad," he says. "Do you still have a bass? Where is it? Is it in the basement?" This whole other side of his father has its hooks in him now. What else doesn't he know about? Maybe his father was in the Army! Maybe he's been to England!

Mr. LaPine smiles at his son. It's an economy smile, a thing Jimmy Carter and Lester Lightbulb would have been proud of. "Miles," he says wearily, "I have no fucking idea."

Miles goes to bed that night feeling full, and puzzled. He's been given instructions. Number one: No telling Mom where we were tonight. She'd get upset about the junk food, and she's got enough to worry about down in Florida with Grammy LaPine, right, buddy? Number two: No telling your sister, when you see her. She'd be jealous of the trip to Friendly's. Number three: No telling classmates. If they hear Miles has had dinner with his teacher, they'll think he's getting special treatment.

As he closes his eyes, Miles tries to think of his mother. In a panic, he realizes he can't remember her face. He tries to reconstruct it in his mind, like one of those games with the felt pieces: Here go the eyes, how about this for a nose, and let's put on a mouth. It doesn't work, though, and it's scary. Is he going crazy? What kind of horrible person can't picture his own mother? He reaches out and fumbles for the brown bear he'd made a point of keeping on the outside of the covers. Then he thinks of Ms. Hansberry, and it's too easy: There are her eyes, her wide mouth, the little U of a nose in between, all where they ought to be. She smells so good, like warm laundry. He imagines her joining them for another dinner, and suddenly he's awake and sitting up.

If she's eating her dinners at Friendly's, she might not have anywhere to go for the holiday.

It's possibly the best idea he's ever had, even better than the Thanksgiving Massacre on the Holiday Wall. He won't take no for an answer, either, not from Ms. Hansberry, not from his father. In this house, the kids always win. Headlights splash his wall. Outside, a car pulls up, crunching the leaves: His sister must be home, finally. Carrie's already announced her plans to be at her friend Amy's for Thanksgiving. It's even more perfect, then, that Ms. Hansberry should join them. To Miles, it's as though this plan were formed in the air above his bed and then lowered onto his brain like a little cloud of genius.

But what about his mother? What if she calls and asks how Thanksgiving was? What will he tell her?

Miles thinks of the instructions for not talking about Friendly's, and there's his answer for Thanksgiving, too. If his mother asks about it, he will tell her what she's expecting to hear: that he and his dad just sat on the couch and drank milk out of the carton.

*the ending isn't
quite there*

Failure to Thrive

Anne wasn't always a social worker. Before that, for the first half of her adult life, she drank. She hit her kids more times than she cares to count, even at this safe distance, twenty years sober and with an advanced degree. When she couldn't afford a babysitter, she dosed them with Benadryl or Nyquil to keep them down through the night while she went to the bars. Once, she found her older boy, Justin, in the bathroom, pouring her bottles into the sink. She shoved him, hard, meaning to hurt him. But Justin tripped on the bathmat, snapping his arm on the edge of the toilet seat. At the hospital, they did not question her story that he'd broken it falling out of a tree, did not make note of the fact that he had older bruises but none of the fresh scrapes you'd expect to see. Anne's grateful to have gotten sober when she did. She can't imagine getting away with that nowadays.

It's a Tuesday in October now, and Anne is on a home visit. She's meeting with Ken and Laurie Aucoin, a longtime foster couple who've taken in a brother and sister, Twon and Shondie Reynolds. The kids are African American, the Aucoins white. In the commonwealth of Massachusetts, foster parents and foster children each have separate representation within the Department of Social Services. This is to avoid any conflict of interest, and also to allow two points of view for comparing notes. It's a rule that wasn't always enforced, but lately it's become something of a mania with Anne's higher-ups. The county's already had two kids die in foster care this year.

Anne is responsible for the Aucoins, the foster parents. The Reynolds kids' file rests with Marvin, a bespectacled, young black man who's just gotten his master's in social work, but looks barely old enough to graduate high school. Marvin has a reputation around the office for quoting rules and statutes to certain old-timers. He was the subordinate worker on the case, but then his lead, Carol Minor, retired last month after a heart episode. Carol was three years younger than Anne. The average burnout rate for social workers in the field is seven years. Anne's been on the job sixteen: Not quite the longest of anyone, but her age puts her in a special class among the field workers. She's become the go-to person for young social workers looking for advice. Except Marvin, of course.

Ken Aucoin has just told Anne and Marvin the banging they hear from outside is Twon hammering some scrap wood together.

"And that's a new hobby for Twon?" says Marvin, taking out the Reynolds kids' case file. Twon is eleven, Shondie twelve. They're ten months apart. Anne wonders if the term "Irish twins" still applies if the kids in question are non-white.

Ken eyes Marvin's file a little nervously, as anyone would. "I don't let him use any power tools," he says.

"It's okay, Ken," says Anne. "We didn't think you would." She smiles at him, smiles being the social worker's precious currency. Ken relaxes a little.

"Still," says Marvin. "When the case nurse gets here, we'll need to bring Twon inside to inspect him for bruises of any kind."

There's an uneasy pause as the older adults look at each other. Marvin may have mastered the rules, but he could use some help with the art of nuance. Anne wonders, not for the first time with this case, if there isn't also something racial going on here.

She knows abusers from the inside out, knows Ken Aucoin isn't one. He has none of the tight-mouthed, close-to-the-vest demeanor of the habitual hitter, nor the too-affable bullshit of the secret pincher/biter/scratcher. Twon, as Carol Minor had written in her reports, is a tense, closed-off kid—a description which thumbnails roughly ninety-eight percent of preadolescent African American males in the DSS system. But both kids are easy around Ken, with none of the weirdly collusive eye contact that goes on between kids and their abusers. Like the looks Anne and Justin used to share whenever they were at someone else's house.

"Marvin," says Anne gently, "why don't you go out and see what Twon's up to? Maybe he needs help with his project."

Marvin eyes her a minute, then heads outside.

"I told the case nurse not to bother, actually," Anne tells the Aucoins. "She had a full schedule already."

Laurie holds her palms up. "It's okay," she says. "Marvin's just being good at his job. You guys have to be careful, especially these days." Anne knows what she's referring to: Just last month, a couple down in Worcester was found renting out their teenaged foster kids for sex.

"Still," says Anne. It's her philosophy that treating everyone as a suspect, every visit, only gets you a shrinking foster-client list.

The Aucoins are the definition of lower-middle-class: Ken works for one of the local oil companies, repairing furnaces and AC systems; Laurie teaches at a middle school in a better town. Their house is a two-story Cape the color of window putty. Ken's been redoing the interior, room by room, since Anne took them on as clients, ten years ago. His weakness for damaged kids is also his weakness as a self-appointed contractor; every new foster kid gets to paint his or her room, and Ken usually ends up making a desk or bedside table to size for that particular kid. As a result, the bedroom Shondie's currently in is carrying nearly a dozen layers of paint, while the kitchen Anne and the Aucoins are sitting in hasn't been updated since the house was built in 1964 or so.

Shondie slides into the room, sock-skating. The first person she goes to, Anne notes, is Laurie.

"Can I have some more paper?" Shondie says.

"Mmmmmaybe," says Laurie. "What's the toll?"

Shondie rolls her eyes—but with a grin, Anne notes—and gives her foster mother a hug. Neither has even glanced at Anne through this routine; no one's looking for signs of approval or disbelief.

"Let's go grab you some paper," says Laurie. The ladies leave the kitchen.

Ken watches them go, his eyes crinkling with love. Then he says to Anne, "We want to adopt the kids."

"Oh," says Anne. Then, realizing this sounds lackluster, amends it to "Oh!" with an exclamation point. Ken and Laurie tried to adopt a little boy years ago—Alex, their first foster child. Like the Reynolds kids, Alex was an orphan, so the Aucoins did the paperwork, filed the petition, had a court date set for their hearing. And then trouble came.

When a foster family files for adoption, DSS is required to place an announcement in the local paper. It's a way of notifying any family members who might wish to claim the child for their own. Never mind that the child might not have been in foster care to begin with, had there been caring family members at the ready, but that's how it is: People only want what they're suddenly told they can't have. Sure enough, a week before the hearing, the dead mother's sister—a woman who hadn't seen her nephew for the last five of his seven years alive—saw the ad, came forward, and claimed the boy. The Aucoins were devastated, of course, and Anne had long wondered if they'd given up on adopting, unable to revisit the land of heartbreak. Now she realizes they've been waiting until the right kids came along.

Ken seems to sense her hesitance about celebrating just yet. "I think these guys showed up, at the time they did, for a reason. They need some permanence in their lives, not a constant damn question mark hanging over their heads: 'When are they gonna start hitting us like Mom did? When are they gonna ship us back to DSS?'"

Anne thinks of her own kids, her wasted opportunities, even after she was sober. Her boys should have been in the foster system, and it's lucky for her they weren't. She leans forward and puts her hand on Ken's hand. It's an inappropriate gesture, not because of any intimacy, but because of the hope it implies. She's glad Marvin's not there, watching her.

"I'll get the paperwork started," she tells Ken Aucoin.

Anne is what the AA people call, derisively, a "dry drunk"—someone who quits on her own, without doing the Twelve Steps: admitting that you're powerless, et cetera. So why did she stop drinking in the first place? Justin had long since stopped pleading with her about her drinking, and he was already hanging with the wrong people after school, getting into the family business, so to speak. Her younger son, David, was still cleaning her up when necessary. She could have gone on that way until her liver collapsed or her heart stopped. But late in the game, she cultivated a drinking buddy, a gal named Susan Espy, who took night classes at the state college in the next town over. One night, Susan paid Anne twenty dollars to go to her class and take notes while Susan went out with some guy from the bar.

Anne, only partially drunk, found the college, found the too-bright classroom, and sat down with the notebook Susan had given her. No one looked at her. She was shaking, and her guts were churning: not from lack of booze, but from a kind of stage fright. It occurred to her that her friend hadn't even told her what class it was. What if Anne were called on? It was a three-hour class, and Anne figured she'd leave at the first break. Then the teacher came in and everyone opened his or her notebook. Anne opened hers and found, written in high, slanty script, a collection of words that, even now, feel to her like incantations: Authority, Evaluation, Assimilation, Transference. There were no explanations of these terms—Anne's friend was a terrible note-taker—but they didn't require any to retain their power. The course turned out to be called Family Systems in Social Work. Anne was hooked.

She went back the next week for another twenty dollars, though she suspected she would've done it for free. Eventually, her friend Susan dropped out and faded away before the term was done. It didn't matter: The next semester, Anne re-enrolled in the course for herself and found that she was suddenly interested in something other than drinking. Because by then she'd discovered the magic formula: *B.A. in Psychology with a Concentration in Social Work*. Twenty years of being a drunk, and nothing to show for it. If she could survive college for four years and sixty credits, she'd be allowed to shape people's lives.

In the car back to the office, Marvin says, "You know you can't do that."

"What?" Though she knows what. Marvin had been there when the Aucoins thanked her for helping with the adoption.

"You can't fill them with promise like that, and you can't be their friend."

"Marvin, dear, let me tell you something. I've been a social worker sixteen years, and a parent for over forty."

"So what, are you double burned-out or triple?" With anyone else at DSS, it would be a joke, gallows humor. Marvin's open-mouthed smile, so full of certainty and contempt, makes it clear that he's really asking this question.

"So I've been through more than you'll ever know, God willing. People in this community look at us and see baby-snatchers. I don't think it's a bad thing to give out a little hope once in a while, and to people who deserve it."

"Well, there's something about Twon I'm not quite liking."

Anne thinks: Is it that he's a little black boy being cared for by a white family? Aloud, she says, "He's pretty closed-off. But then, who wouldn't be, after being chewed up like an ear of corn?"

"That's not it. His things that he builds? They don't make sense."

"Marvin, the boy's eleven."

"No, that's just it: They're boxes, and they're impressive and symmetrical, like something a pretty capable grownup would make. But there are no holes, and they don't open. What kind of a kid makes cubes out of wood? Raises kind of a flag for me."

Anne thinks back to her conversation with Ken Aucoin about adopting the kids. A troubled boy needs a father. God knows that might have made a difference with her own sons.

"You have a lot more visits today?" she asks Marvin.

He sighs, showing a rare sign of weariness. "Two." He'll be lucky to get these done in time for 5:00, and if there's one thing DSS hates more than dead foster kids, it's paying overtime.

"Well, how about this: I'm in the office the rest of the day. I'll put together the report for the Aucoin visit." She smiles at him, just being the kindly older lady from the office. "I'll incorporate your concerns."

"Okay," says Marvin cautiously. "Thank you for that."

"Don't mention it," says Anne.

At home that night, Anne goes through the mail over a dinner of ramen noodles, mashed potatoes, and broccoli. The food is courtesy of David, her younger son, who's back living with her after trying his hand at married life. He's been here only four months, yet in that time Anne has put on seven pounds. It can't be a coincidence.

When he was little, David used to clean her up in the morning, so she could get up and go to work at her pharmacy job. He'd burrow under her bedcovers from the bottom of the bed, rubbing her feet and calling, "Calgon, take me away!" When he was six, he knew how to make her coffee the way she liked, as well as her drinks. (This was back when she still bothered to mix her drinks.) The day she broke Justin's arm, it was David who'd told her Justin was in the bathroom, pouring her vodka down the sink. David was, she now knows, a classic caretaker. He's not alive if he's not rescuing somebody, particularly seriously messed-up women. His wife, Julie, was the most together person he ever went with, which surprised Anne when he started seeing her, and not at all when he finally left her. When you don't need to play Batman every night and remove a beautiful girl from the clutches of her abusive dad or drug problem or creepy ex-husband, a stable marriage can seem pointless.

Now David stands in the kitchen, her thirty-five-year-old boy, spooning out mashed potatoes from a pot on the stove-top. Beside him, the window is frosted with starchy steam.

"Ask me how many," David says.

"Okay," says Anne. "How many?"

"Four."

"Wow, pretty good." What he means is, he nailed four perps today. David is a patrolman for the city of Rollstone. He is its tallest, most aggressive enemy of the criminal element, as he calls them. He's also six credits shy of his criminal justice degree, which has kept him firmly in the rookie limbo of squad cars and arrest reports for the last decade. A degree would enable him to begin the long climb up the chain of command. Anne knows this is exactly why he's taken so long to finish the degree. He wants to spend his entire police career as a foot soldier. He has no ambition to manage, oversee, or interrogate. He just wants to catch the bad guys and put them in jail.

"Sit down, crazy-pants," Anne says. "Eat with me."

"All right, let me just . . . ," and he trails off, looking toward the door at the front of the kitchen.

"What?" says Anne, though she already knows what.

"Shh."

And then she hears it, too: not just the neighborhood dogs barking, but a sound like torrential rain at the front of the house. But it's not rain. It's the sound, so familiar now, of handfuls of gravel against vinyl siding.

Justin is paying a visit.

Justin, until a year ago, was the one who'd never left home. He never married, though he'd been committed to chemicals longer than Anne can remember. No, that's not true: She has clear snapshots of herself holding him down, pouring the cough syrup down his throat at various ages—when he was little, to get him to sleep through the night; when he was older, to calm the awful hurricane he'd become every few days, when he would leave school, or attack a teacher, or climb a grocery store. These are their family photos, these memories, and she's grateful that they exist only in the three brains that took them. Now she knows what Justin is, or was: A 296.40 in the *DSM-IV-TR:* Bipolar with Hypomanic Episode. Only, he long ago figured out he preferred the white fury and energy of mania to the black, sea-soaked-clothing, downward drag of depression. There's no additional code or decimal in the *DSM* for what Justin is when you factor in the basement-made chemistry he pumps into his veins. The closest dictionary definition might be Monster.

After a long moment, the gravel storm ceases. Scuffling from the front, then a sort of digging sound. He's on the front stoop. Then silence falls on the house like a tarp. There have been noisy visitations for months, but this is the closest Justin has come to the house in the year since she finally gave him the ultimatum: Get help or get out. Anne looks to David, but he's frozen beside the table, white-knuckling a chair. He looks like he's five years old again, caught in the volcanic heat of one of his big brother's epic rages.

There's a tiny enclosed porch between the inner kitchen door and the outer door to the house, like a mudroom. Anne moves for the inner door.

"Mom, don't!" shouts David, calling after her. He's still holding onto the chair. For all his size—and this is a big, strong guy who tangles with desperate, messed-up people all day for a living—he's still terrified by his older brother. When he was little and Justin would go into his rages, throwing plates and silverware, David would crawl between the couch and the wall and hunch there until it was over: Duck and Cover. This is probably why Anne never hit David when he was a kid, not once. And Anne is terrified, too, but she's driven by something more. She needs to see how close Justin actually got this time.

He still has a room here, his bed made up, top right corner of the covers pulled down diagonally, as if he's just in the bathroom, brushing his teeth. Not that he had that many teeth left when Anne last saw him.

Anne's kept tabs on Justin via David and the various cops she knows through work. Justin's spent his year squatting with various lowlifes, Rollstone these days having no shortage of abandoned buildings. A few nights a week, no matter what's in his veins, he manages to find the wherewithal to come stand at the bottom of his mother's yard, throwing gravel from the street at her front door. It might have something to do with the bags of McDonald's food she's been leaving for him in the mailbox. Which, reaching the outer door, she realizes she forgot tonight. She was wrapped up with the Aucoin report, and with getting the adoption paperwork started, Marvin be damned.

Anne clicks on the mudroom light and pulls open the front door, David behind her, yelling, "Mom, don't!" But the stoop, the yard, the driveway: all empty.

"See?" she says, turning to David. But he's looking past her. She turns to see what he sees.

On the door, her firstborn baby has carved a message:

CUNT

Next day, at the office, Marvin knocks on the fabric-covered wall of Anne's cubicle. "Got a minute?"

Anne looks at the pile of case folders on her desk. Each caseworker is supposed to have no more than twelve cases. At the Rollstone office of the Department of Social Services, there are currently eighteen cases per worker. "Maybe less than that," says Anne.

Marvin comes in and sits in the chair by her desk. "Your report," he says. "On the Aucoin visit? I don't feel it fully captures the facts."

The phone on her desk rings. The caller ID says ROLLSTONE CITY OF.

"I have to take this," she says, hoping not to appear too grateful for the interruption. She picks it up, watching Marvin go stomping off through the office, his head bobbing, receding, then disappearing among the maze of cubicle walls. There's no way she's allowing him back into the Aucoins' house, never mind attending the adoption proceedings.

David's on the phone. "I just wanted to make sure you're okay," he says.

"Me? Why?"

"I just talked to Mikey Juarez, patrols over on the west side. Did you know there's a warrant out for him?" Justin, he means.

"I hadn't heard that."

"He hurt someone this time, Mom. A kid. He was shaking school kids down for lunch money. This one fifth grader wouldn't give it up. Justin threw him against a tree."

Anne finds herself reaching for a cigarette, though there's no smoking in the office, and Anne hasn't owned cigarettes in three years now, her last vice to shed. She settles for holding a pen between her fingers. "Is he okay? The kid, I mean?"

"He's in the hospital with a broken collarbone. You know, this town will put up with a lot, but not when a kid's involved. And Mom?"

"Yeah?"

"If you see him, any sign of him, you need to tell me right away. No kidding around."

"I know."

That night, when she pulls up at the mailbox at the front of the yard and takes out the mail, she puts in the McDonald's bag, just as she has every night for the last two years—except last night. Inside, as always, is the food, along with an envelope of bills, softened from the heat of the burgers. This time, she's written on the envelope:

$60 MORE IS THE MOST I CAN GIVE
BUT LEAVE KIDS ALONE!
AND CUT YOUR HAIR. THEY ARE LOOKING FOR YOU.

Later, eating another of David's starch-fests, they hear the dogs barking, but that's it. No rain of stones, no footsteps. When David goes out to check, no new message has been added to her door.

The following week's visit at the Aucoins', she doesn't bring Marvin but does bring the nurse. It's a compromise with herself. Anne sits at the table with Laurie—Ken is stuck at work—and goes through the Petition for Adoption with her. Twon and Shondie take turns in the bathroom with the nurse.

"Now line four," says Anne, "you need to check that off: The kids have resided with you for more than six months. Then we have to find a notary to—" and suddenly her client is sobbing.

"No, no," says Anne. "It's okay. You probably had more paperwork for the foster care."

"It's not that," says Laurie. "It's these kids." And she breaks off in more sobs.

Anne's heart dips. Jesus: Is she backing out?

"It's okay," says Anne. "Everyone gets overwhelmed when they see the form. It's like it's suddenly *real* now, right?"

"That's not it," says Laurie. "I just—we've been at this point before, with Alex. How can I feel like it's not gonna get yanked out from under us again? It's exactly how I felt then, and also when we were applying for our mortgage. Isn't that awful?"

"You're putting a lot of your life in someone else's hands," says Anne.

"Right, and these are human souls. It shouldn't feel like you're acquiring something, or that it's a thing to be taken away from you. And is that any way for a kid to start a new life? Does childbirth ever feel like that? You have kids, right? Wasn't it anything but a transaction?"

Anne smiles, but doesn't answer. She was knocked out for both boys' births. She woke up in her hospital bed, feeling exhausted, torn-up, bored-out, with a little warm thing, still smelling of blood, on her chest. It was not a transaction, no; it was an extraction.

Twon and Shondie burst into the kitchen, filling the room with their young, uncompromised energy, looking for drinks and snacks like regular kids in a regular home. The nurse ducks in and gives Anne a thumbs-up. Then Shondie goes into the living room to work on drawings, while Twon heads out to build with Ken's seemingly inexhaustible supply of wood.

Laurie Aucoin is not really asking about childbirth. Here is a woman who miscarried five times and has been a foster mother for more kids than even the most seasoned welfare fraud would put up with. She wants to be told she's finally going to be a mother.

Anne, against all her training, against her sober judgment, takes her client's hand and makes a promise she can't possibly guarantee.

Heading back to the office, Anne stops at a stoplight by a half-deserted shopping center, one of several in Rollstone. A trio of teenagers takes turns riding a shopping cart around like a chariot. This place, before it was a plaza, was a ball field. Anne played softball here when she was in high school. Later, when the kids were little and they paved it over, it housed her favorite liquor store, the one that sold vodka and gin in two-liter, generic bottles. Sitting in her car, she's startled to find herself thinking of drinks. The wetness of them, the sweetness cut with the almost antiseptic burn of the alcohol—if you're mixing, that is.

The shopping-cart riders walk their cart up toward the road, to build up speed, and that's when Anne realizes she's been looking at her son. She hasn't seen Justin in natural light in more than a year. He's taken his mother's advice. In place of his long greasy pile of hair is a white skull covered in patches and fresh scars that are visible from where Anne sits. It's as if he's tried to do the whole thing with a disposable razor, which is probably not far off. At six-eight, Justin is taller than his younger brother. Standing on the back of the cart with his arms stretched out, back arched, tattered black duster hanging from his bones, he looks like the skeleton of a bat. The people with him appear to be a man and a woman, though with their piles of hair and layers of clothes and grime, it's hard to tell.

Justin's cart tips, and he goes tumbling to the pavement. Anne feels a sudden hitch in her chest, like when you trip over a stray tree root. She's partly worried about her son being injured, yes, but she's also just realized she has no memory to match this sight. She's never seen Justin riding on a shopping cart, not ever in his life, though surely he must have done it, probably hundreds of times. Doesn't every kid? But most of the child-related memories Anne has are either of things she regrets doing or of things that happened to kids she's known on the job. Everything else is lost, forever, it seems, in the black hole of her drinking years. Or black lake, as it were.

Anne wants to pull over and warn her son to get the hell out of sight, that his brother and his patrol buddies are probably looking for him. After rolling on the ground, Justin finally gets to his feet, laughing. Then he turns to the road and immediately locks onto his mother, as if he's known all along she was right there, watching. A car behind Anne blares its horn—the light is green, there's no one in front of her now—but she can't move. Justin smiles, the mouthful of rot clear even from this distance, and points right at her. Something cold flashes in her gut. The car behind her beeps again and she floors it.

At home that night, she and David sit in the living room, watching television post-dinner (spaghetti with a side of corn). She hasn't said anything about seeing Justin today. She knows she should. David could help him, or could get him somewhere for help, anyway. But if he's picked up, he'll either attack his apprehender (assaulting an officer), or he'll have something on him that's way beyond the scope of misdemeanor-class substances. He'd have to do time, then, and she can't do that to her boy. He didn't make himself this way, not without her help. She is a part of this thing.

Law & Order is on. In the show, the wealthy playwright, who's just been discovered as the real murderer of his wife, runs down the street. Our detective heroes give chase while the uniformed cops watch helplessly. Just when it seems the murderer might get away, the younger detective make a last-ditch leap and tackles him.

"That's gonna be you," says Anne, nudging David.

"Everyone says this show's unpredictable, but it's got a pattern," he says. "Ninety percent of the time, it's the rich person. If there's no rich person, it's the mother. And if there's a rich mother, then it's her, hundred percent of the time."

He's teasing her, but he's also redirecting. For a martyr, he sure hates attention. It was Justin who always craved it. One time, when he was four, Justin picked a different type of facial tissue at the grocery store. He spent the rest of the day asking, "How do you like those Kleenex, Mama? Did I pick a good kind?" Anne wonders: What would be the appropriate praise for Justin now? "You're a terrifying vampire"?

Anne pats David on the leg. "I'm proud of you, you know."

"I can't be the only one who's figured out *Law & Order.*"

"Oh, quit it. You're a hell of a patrolman, and you're still on your way. Just don't stop, okay? Don't be afraid to go to the next level just because it might change you. Change is good."

David looks at her. "Today I caught someone I've caught four times before." He glances at the TV. "I'm starting not to believe that people can change." Anne looks at him, and there's a smirk curling the corners of his mouth, his still-babyish mouth. For the second time that day, something cold flashes in the pit of herself. This man, this sweet, overgrown boy, has never displayed even a hint of cynicism.

At the same time, Anne wants to say: Really? What about me? I was a horrible person, and now I help other people. I've just found new parents for a set of lost, unwanted kids. Is that all for nothing?

Then the cinder block comes crashing through the front window.

"Down! Down!" yells David. He throws Anne to the floor, turning her face toward the carpet, away from the attack. Then he's off her. When Anne looks up, David is by the window, back pressed against the adjacent wall. He makes himself flat, almost part of the wall, and he dips his head forward to take a quick look out the window.

"Fuck it," he spits, and he tromps back through the living room, glass shards crunching under his sneakers. Anne hears one of the kitchen drawers open and close, then the front door. Anne stays lying on the floor, unsure what to do next. The cinder block is not a cinder block. Rather, it is her gray, metal mailbox, a long piece of firewood jammed in it to give the weight necessary to take out a picture window. Paper plumes from the mouth of the mailbox, red and white and yellow, like a child's drawings of flames.

Anne recognizes it as the McDonald's bag she put in there earlier tonight. She sits up, suddenly realizing she needs to get rid of that bag.

"What's that?" It's too late: David is back in the living-room doorway. He has a gun in his hand. It's his old service revolver, the one he had before his buddies got him something more modern, as if there were degrees of lethality.

"Davey," Anne says. "You are not going to shoot your brother."

He tucks the gun in the back of his waistband. Then he strides over and picks up the decapitated mailbox.

"Davey," she says again.

He extracts the log and pulls out one, two, three—five McDonald's bags.

"What the fuck?" he says. He uncurls one of the bags. "'Cut your hair,'" he reads, "'they're looking for you.'" Then he unbunches another one. "'Please get help. You looked terrible today.'" This was tonight's bag. David's lips draw back in revulsion. "'I love you Justy'?" He looks at her with something like pity, and shakes his head.

"I know," says Anne. "I know, I know."

"Where do I even begin? So, what, you've clearly seen him recently—after you knew about the warrant—and didn't tell anyone? He hurt a *kid,* Mom. Your Justy. Isn't your whole job to protect kids? And money, you've been giving him money, so that's great. You know that's aiding and abetting at this point."

"Are you going to arrest me?"

"Of course I'm not. I do need to know where you saw him and what he looks like now."

"Okay. It was on Main Ave., that brand new mini-mall. He was coming out of the CVS."

David shakes his head. "Crank-head probably stole some old lady's prescription."

"Right, probably. He had, what, shoulder-length hair, dyed white. Denim jacket."

David nods. "Okay, good." He heads back toward his bedroom.

"Where are you going?"

"Getting my cell. I'm gonna call this in to Mikey Juarez." He's smiling, jazzed to be doing police work. Brother or no, David is in his element now. The terror that usually grips him at his brother's "visits" is gone.

Seeing Anne's face, he suddenly softens.

"They won't hurt him, Mom, unless he hurts them first. They'll hold him downtown, no prison stuff yet, let him clean out for a few days, get his brains unscrambled for the court date. It'll be good for him. Maybe we can talk the vic's family into seeking lesser charges."

"David," says Anne, holding her hand out. "Your gun."

He blushes, a little boy caught with brown sugar around his mouth. "I wasn't gonna shoot him."

"Well, give it here. I'll put it back for you. Where do you keep it?"

He hands her the piece. "Where I know you'd never find it," he says with a half-grin. "In the baking cabinet."

* * *

The Aucoins just don't know how to thank her.

It's what she does, Anne tells them.

It's a Friday afternoon, and she's just presented the Aucoins with a completed, notarized Petition for Adoption. The court date is Monday morning, at which point the adoption will be official. It's not a scheduled visit today, so Anne didn't feel the need to inform Marvin. She's been avoiding him as much as possible lately.

This event should have been ninety days in the making, red tape dispensing, as it does, no more than an inch at a time. Anne has made it happen in thirty. She fought for this one, held it up as a case DSS can actually publicize. Can you not picture this in the paper? she asked her bosses. Instead of another "DSS takes kids away" story or "Baby dies on DSS's watch"? Indeed she has a photographer from the *Rollstone Sentinel* coming to the Aucoins' house Monday afternoon to photograph the new family.

The photographer was her second call to the *Sentinel*. Her first was to place the required Intent to Adopt notice, the same thing that tripped up the Aucoins ten years ago. And Anne did place the notice, but in her haste, she might not have placed it in the proper place. It's supposed to go on the same page with the police blotter and the court appearance notices. But Anne might have gotten the adoption notice placed somewhere deep, deep inside the sports scores.

The adults sit in the kitchen: Anne, Ken, and Laurie. No nurse this time, no Marvin. Anne would like this one all to herself.

Twon comes in. He's small for his age, wouldn't tower over most eight-year-olds. Failure to Thrive is the technical term. Raised on a Diet of Shit Sandwiches is Anne's preferred nomenclature.

"Hey, you," says Laurie. Twon grunts. "There's more of those yogurt smoothies you like in the fridge."

He grunts again, but moves for the refrigerator and gets himself a bottle.

Twon turns and regards Anne with cold eyes. She flinches and thinks immediately what Marvin would say if he were here. But Marvin's just a kid himself. He didn't raise two boys. Anne knows this one needs a little time, and a lot of love and patience, which he's getting by the ton here.

"Knock knock," says Twon.

"Who's there," says Anne.

"Interrupting goldfish," says Twon.

Anne knows already this is not how the joke is supposed to go—the line is "interrupting cow," and Twon is then supposed to blurt "Moo!" while she's saying, "Interrupting cow who?" But she winks at him and says, "Interrupting goldfish wh—"

"Stop interrupting me, asshole!" screams Twon.

"Twon!" yells Ken, and he's on his feet.

"Okay," says Anne coolly, though she knows this is not okay. She does note that Ken has not left his side of the table, nor are his hands made into fists. That's a good sign.

"Whoa," says Twon, and he grabs the sides of his own head. With his hands, he dances his close-cropped noggin around like a balloon in a windstorm.

"Twon?" says Laurie. "Sweetie?" She looks concerned, but there's something in her voice—a lack of panic—that suggests this is not a new scene. How many times has the boy done this before? wonders Anne.

"Hey, stupid!" snaps Shondie. "They're talking to you." She looks at Anne and rolls her eyes, as if her brother has merely burped at the dinner table.

Twon stops and blinks, looking around the kitchen. "Whoa," he says again. "Where am I? Who am I?"

Anne smiles at his performance. His face flickers through a few different emotions, like a tentative cable signal. Finally, a smile comes on. Okay, Anne thinks: Smiling is good. It's the ones who don't smile, or can't, that you want to worry about. She wishes Marvin could see this, so she could teach him the difference. The Aucoins are clearly relieved. The storm having passed, they're smiling again.

"That was pretty nutsy, my friend," says Ken.

"Ah," says Twon, waving him off, face scrunched up like an old pro who doesn't need the praise. Of course, he's also enjoying the attention. Shondie still looks annoyed with the whole performance.

Anne packs her briefcase, watching Twon as he heads out to work on one of his wood projects. Thank God for the wood, she thinks; a kid like that needs something to pour himself into. More than ever, she's convinced Twon is where he needs to be. He needs this family, possibly even more than it needs him.

Sunday night, David's criminal justice textbooks are stacked on Anne's kitchen table. A final exam tomorrow night, and then he'll have his degree. He can move onward and upward through the ranks, gaining more responsibility and command. Naturally, he's sitting on the couch beside Anne, leaving the books to study themselves, apparently.

There's a reality show on. Families ride terrifying zip lines down mountains, into valleys, to win points and secure a shared spot for the next round of torture.

On the couch, David sips his soda. "Quiet tonight."

He means that while dogs have barked here and there, it's not like the other nights. Also, nothing's come crashing through the window. This is possibly because Anne left a stack of homemade sandwiches in the new mailbox, along with two hundred dollars. To head off the questions that must be formulating in David's mind, Anne says, "Why aren't you studying?"

"What? I know this shit backwards and forwards," David says. "Sorry: stuff."

"You can say shit, you know," Anne says. "You're thirty-five."

"Okay. Shit."

As soon as he says it she wishes she could erase it. It doesn't sound right, coming out of his mouth. She doesn't like it.

He grins. "Shit, shit, shit, shit."

Anne forces a smile. "Okay, all done? Good. Now go." She shuts off the TV.

David glares at her, then goes to the table. He slumps into the chair with a huff, like an irritated nine-year-old. "Since when do you care when I do my homework anyway?" he says into his books. "Isn't it a little late in life for that?"

He's just being snippy, but it stings anyway.

"It's never too late," she says. They both hear the extra weight in her voice, and David looks up, squinting at his mother as Anne wipes at her eyes. "People can change, you know."

"Okay, okay," he says, head back down, facing the books. "Whatever you say, boss."

She would like to remind him that it used to be her, sitting at that same table with a stack of books after a long day at work. She would like to remind him that she stopped drinking when he was ten, for Christ's sake, that she was awake and present during his teenaged years. Even the times when college, and then grad school, and then her new job kept her too busy for the fine details of daily life, still: awake and present.

Instead, she gets up and goes to the kitchen and makes him a pot of coffee. Because that's what you do.

The adoption goes perfectly. Fifteen minutes of proceedings, and Twon and Shondie have a new mom and dad, and a new last name. Marvin is there in a suit and shiny new shoes, and he nods and smiles with the events, even though Anne imagines he'll give her an earful later about shutting him out of the process. Shondie declines the judge's offer to bang the gavel, but Twon leaps at the chance, tapping it several times, lightly, all around the top of the judge's podium, just as Anne knew he would, saying, "Judge, your house here is falling apart all over the place." Everyone laughs, the judge loudest of all. Twon looks at them, pleased with himself, but never breaking whatever character he's being.

They have lunch back at the house, Anne and Marvin and all four Aucoins. After lunch, the photographer will be here from the newspaper. Anne and Marvin's boss, Gloria Norrell, will be there. Gloria is not known for stepping into the field, so this is a big deal indeed. During lunch, Marvin leans in to Anne. "I'm sorry I was such a stick-in-the-mud," he says. "You were right. This is the best thing for these kids."

Anne pats his hand. "You should never apologize for asking questions." Even so, she feels herself glowing on the inside. Wanting to share her high, she says, "I like your shoes. I like the stitching across the toe there."

Marvin crosses his leg so his foot is between them. "Thanks!" he says. Then he rolls his eyes, embarrassed. "When I was in high school, I always wanted a pair of cap toes." There's still a sticker on the sole, and Anne realizes he bought new shoes just for today. They're going to be okay, she and Marvin.

After lunch, Shondie is at work at the table, drawing a picture of the new, official Aucoin family. They stand in a tight formation before the house, all big purple heads and little gray bean-bodies. Everyone smiles except for Twon, who's got a flat line for a mouth. Next to Twon's leg is a brown lump.

"What's Twon got there?" Anne asks Shondie. "That a puppy?"

Shondie rolls her eyes; silly Anne or crazy Twon, it's not clear. "That's one of his stupid birdhouses."

Anne looks at Ken as if to say, *That's* what he's been making?

"First I've heard a name put to them," says Ken. "Good to know." From outside comes the sound of Twon's hammer.

"He doesn't like to talk about them," says Shondie. "He's always angry 'cause they never work."

"Maybe there's some kind of kit we can get him," Laurie says.

"I don't know," says Anne. "In some way, he may come to value the work more than the end result." The two grownups nod at this.

"I hadn't thought of that," says Laura. "I'm just thinking of his frustration, but you're right: There is a bigger picture."

Anne shrugs. "It's just the kind of stuff they drill into us at DSS." She glances at Marvin, still half expecting a sneer, but he's looking at her with something like admiration. Even without his approval, she would delight at a moment like this. Being the expert, guiding with a firm but gentle hand. It's a high, better than any drink or drug she's ever known.

"No," says Shondie. "You should get him what Laurie said, a regular-style birdhouse kit. I keep telling you guys, Twon's crazy."

Out in the yard, Twon kneels before a low, flat-topped tree stump, hammering at the box that sits atop it with long yet delicate taps. He's dressed in a nice pair of navy corduroys, with a pink-and-yellow polo shirt. He's wearing the new sneakers Anne bought him for the adoption hearing. His box, fashioned of scrap wood of varying pieces, is admirably box-shaped. It has corners and edges that look right to Anne's admittedly untrained eye. It might be big enough to hold a grapefruit inside, or a little boy's treasure collection. From where Anne's standing, she can't imagine why he would be dissatisfied with his work.

It's a man-made miracle, a December day like this. Anne, in her thin sweater and long skirt, feels only slightly chilly. She approaches Twon and his work-stump on gentle feet. "Hey there, Twon," she says. "Whatcha building?"

You learn to walk and talk carefully in this job. Everything you do is a potential threat, a mark on someone's delicate psyche, something she certainly didn't know for the first half of her life. When she asks Twon what he's doing, for example, she doesn't use the word "making," which is benign and nonspecific; anyone can "make" something, and making isn't a particularly concrete concept: You can make a thing, yes, but you can also make time, make plans, make pretend. "Building," though, that gives the impression of accomplishment, skill, ability. With that one word, she is giving Twon credit, something he's been deprived of all his life.

"I'm making a fucking box," says Twon. "What's it look like?"

Anne tries not to show her shock. The worst thing to do with a kid like this is let him know he's rattled you.

"What is it, though?" she says. "Like a box for your stuff? Or is it a present for somebody?"

"It's a birdhouse," he says, and he begins to hammer again.

Now they're getting somewhere. Twon is not one for specifics.

"I used to build birdhouses with my dad when I was little," Anne tells him. She doesn't mention how drunk her dad would get while they were down in the basement, or that the only reason he'd go down there in the first place was because it was his excuse for visiting his stash of rye.

"You had a dad?" says Twon.

"I did. He's dead now."

Twon snorts. "Lucky." Anne doesn't know if this means lucky for having a dad, or lucky he's dead. Twon hammers a new nail into the box. Even his nail-spacing is admirable. The boy is a woodworking prodigy. Anne sits down beside the stump, to let Twon know she's not intimidated by his tough-guy act, and that they're going to have a real conversation. There's a rasping sound coming from the stump, or just behind it. Anne wonders if the thing's full of termites, or if the stump's situated over a chipmunk nest.

"Big day, huh?" says Anne. "Banging the gavel, new family, newspaper photographer coming."

"It's a'ight."

"Just all right?" she says. "You know, Twon, sometimes we don't—" and she stops. The rasping sound is there again. It's definitely a woody sound. Anne scoots back a bit on the chilly grass.

"Anyway, if there's anything you need to tell me, ever, you can do that. Even though I won't be your family's social worker anymore."

Twon looks up. "You won't?"

"You guys are good now. I have to go help some other kids who aren't as lucky as you and your sister."

Twon lays down his hammer. "Why you guys gotta put us with a white family anyway?" he says. "What the fuck?"

Anne looks away. She wants to deprive his anger of its power. "You, my friend, are with the very best family we knew," she says, and it's true. "Do your new mom and dad love you?"

"They say they do."

"Do they take good care of you?"

"Yeah."

"Do they ever hurt you, like other people in your life have?"

"No."

"Okay, then."

"Ken had a beer last night. After I went to bed. I heard the cap coming off the bottle. You might want to look into that."

Anne smiles. "Tell you what. How about if I drop by some time to check on you guys? Like a friend."

"Okay." Twon looks at his box, cutting the wood with his eyes. Then he picks it up off the stump and hands it to Anne.

"It's very nice," says Anne.

"You can keep it," he says, not looking up at her. "Since you're not gonna be our social worker anymore."

Anne feels the water pushing at her eyes. She swallows, hard, and looks at the box, turning it over in her hands. "It's beautiful, Twon. Thank you. I'll keep it always."

"A'ight. I hope that bird likes it as much."

"Well, *I* like it," she says. Then she realizes what's wrong with Twon's birdhouses: There's no hole in this box. Should she point this out? On one hand, there's the make-him-feel-competent thing. On the other hand, he's frustrated by his birdhouses not working, and there's a very clear, demonstrable reason: no bird-hole.

"Hey Twon," Anne says offhandedly. "I think any bird would be honored to have this for a house."

"Okay."

"So I guess I have a question: If I find a bird who wants to live in here, what should I tell him when he wants to get in?"

Twon takes a step back and tilts his head, looking at her in a rather birdlike fashion himself. "What do you mean?" he says. "What 'get in'?"

"The door," says Anne. "A birdhouse needs a door, don't you think?"

Twon shakes his head, as if Anne is an idiot. "He's already in."

"Sorry?"

"I said he's already in there."

Anne looks at Twon, who is not smiling, and she gives the box a little shake. Something shifts inside, and then Anne hears the rasping sound she thought was bugs, or chipmunks under the stump. And now she can hear it's not a rasping at all. It's a fluttering.

"Twon?" she says, and then, looking past him for the first time, sees the discarded birdhouses by the side of the plastic tool shed. There must be two-dozen solid cubes of mismatching wood grain, piled like stones.

Twon smiles now, the sweetest, most genuine smile Anne's ever seen him give. "The one I caught yesterday lasted a hour. That's my best yet! How long you think this one will go?"

In Anne's house, it is breezy, loud with the crisp night air. This has nothing to do with the front window, which David had replaced for her. No, the December breeze that stampedes in, sniffing out the warm corners of Anne's house, is from the front door, which stands wide open.

It is eight o'clock. David is at his final exams and won't be back until late. She's counting on it. Both her boys, come to think of it, can be counted on for something.

The Aucoins' newspaper photo couldn't have gone better. Gloria Norrell showed up just in time and hugged her "two star social workers." Everyone gathered in front of the house, the sky a bright yet sunless winter-white the photographer said couldn't have been more perfect. "Sky like this, nobody needs to squint," he explained to Anne, who was standing beside him, still holding the box Twon had given her. She was scared to put it down, lest anyone else pick it up and feel the fluttering from inside. "No kooky shadows on anyone."

The parents stood in the back, each with their arms wrapped criss-cross, like sweater arms, over the chest of the kid in front. Anne and Marvin flanked the family, a pair of guardian angels. Gloria Norrell stood just off to the left, beside Anne. Gloria had her body turned slightly, arms gesturing toward the big, happy group, as if she were presenting the winners at a livestock contest. After a few shots, Twon yelled, "Ooh, wait!" Then he ran over to Anne and grabbed the box she was still holding. Anne hadn't heard or felt a fluttering in several minutes.

"Gotta borrow this."

Then he got right back into position, Ken's arms once again slung around him, and held up his newest birdhouse. The photographer snapped more pictures.

"Careful, Twon," said Ken. "Some contractor's gonna see that and offer you a job." And everyone laughed, including Twon, who chuckled with the lower half of his face. His eyes remained unchanged—so alert yet so distant—and Anne had an image of this boy taller, perched atop a speeding shopping cart, black coat draped around his body like a set of bat's wings.

Out in front of Anne's house now, the new mailbox sits open, empty, lid folded down in front of its maw like a tongue. The whole setup—foodless, cashless mailbox; open front doors; every light on in the house—should be taunting, infuriating, irresistible. Through the front window, Justin's chemical-starved, misfiring brain will see his rotten, neglectful mother sitting on the couch, watching TV. What's the rule about vampires? That they can't enter a house without being invited? Anne's front door is wedged open with an oven mitt.

She hasn't got a plan so much as a scene: a woman on a couch, waiting for her sons to come home in the proper order. That's as far as she's gotten. That's not true: She has David's old service revolver in her lap. No idea what David will do when he comes home and finds the mess he's going to find. She hopes he'll see the upside. He should never want to spend another night in this house. He should finally see there's nowhere for him to go but onward and upward. This is her last, possibly only, gift to her good son.

After the photograph at the Aucoins' today, she went back to the office and left her case file on Twon and Shondie Reynolds in a sealed envelope on Marvin's chair. There's also a long note in there, explaining what he needs to say to Gloria Norrell in order to direct all culpability toward Anne and away from himself. Anne knows now, she didn't merely invite Twon into the Aucoins' house—she shoved him over the threshold and nailed the door shut. Like throwing a kid against a toilet, that's not really an "oops!" situation. And maybe it's not too late for Twon, but what if it is? What happens when he gets bored with birds? It raises a question for Anne: If she's not a social worker, the nice lady who comes to the houses and asks all the questions and gives the gentle advice, what is she? It's a question she hasn't been willing to ask, never mind answer, since she sat down in a psychology class and opened her own, clean notebook.

It's a shitty, drowning thing to have spent decades thinking you're changing, growing, only to realize, in one horrible instant, that you've stayed the same, stunted person all along. She takes a swig of the gin she bought on the way home from the office. After all these years, it doesn't taste the way she remembers. It tastes cold, clinical. It's like someone liquefied a hospital and bottled it. She can't remember why she loved this stuff so much. Still, she feels good and dull, and if you're giving yourself up to fate, that is the state to be in. Chain yourself to the rock and wait for the dragon. David's revolver sits heavy in her lap, the grip warming in her hand. She thought about removing only herself from the home, but she can't leave Justin behind in the world. She made him the thing he is; she has to take him with her. If he were to magically straighten out tomorrow, after all these years, it would be a victory over chemistry and nothing else. He would have no idea how to live as a person. It would be like sending a ten-year-old boy out alone into the world: funny in the movies, not so much in real life.

She feels bad about using David's gun for this. She always pictured it hanging framed in his office, years in the future, when he'd be lieutenant or captain.

The television is on, but muted. She wants to hear every sound from outside. The neighborhood dogs start in. Rabbit? Raccoon? Anne knows it's neither. And then it begins: She doesn't see him yet, but now she can definitely hear him, scuffling up the front walk. She pictures him in his coat, the darkness of him swallowing even the moonlight, a shadow of a shadow. She takes a quick last swig from the bottle, remembers pouring medicine down her boy's slender throat. Remembers him gagging on the harsh green syrup. The calmness that would draw across that angry brow, smoothing it like a trowel. The peace.

A creak in the kitchen, and she draws out the gun, holding it up as steadily as she can. She takes a breath, wishes for one last, last swig, and prepares to make everything all better.

His darkness fills the doorway. He says, "Hey, I—" and Anne squeezes her finger and fires. The sound deafens her, like a blanket over her head. It shakes her tears back into her eyes. She keeps firing until he's dropped, three huge blasts. She opens her eyes, but doesn't look at him; she can't. So she looks at the floor instead, his feet just poking into the edge of her peripheral vision. They look so much smaller than she remembers. She's made it better, though, given him his peace, and that's all that matters. Then she realizes the feet are wearing shiny, black, cap-toe Oxfords. And there beside them is the package she left on Marvin's chair.

Terrible, unfair ending. Lots of nice things in this story, but the last page or so is a horrid, overdone misstep

Depot Island

His mother sounded small over the phone. Miles couldn't tell if it was because she'd been drinking, or because of all the trucks grumbling back and forth outside his motel window. It was a wet towel of a night in North Carolina, the 3rd of July, 1982. Miles LaPine was newly twelve. It had been a week since Miles' dad had left Miles and his sixteen-year-old sister, Carrie, in their motel room at the two-square-mile truck stop called Depot Island. It was the summer before Miles was due to start seventh grade. They were supposed to be on a nice two-week road trip from Massachusetts to Orlando and back, a first and last chance for a divorced, disgraced father to make good. Now Miles sat on the motel bed, dangling his feet as he told his mother about the big day he hadn't had at the Magic Kingdom.

"And Pirates of the Caribbean, of course. Whoo, that was something." It sounded fake; he prayed she wouldn't ask for more detail.

"Tell me all about it," said Kate LaPine. There was wine in her voice. All her syllables were mushy, slanted. Miles fumbled for one of the brochures he'd grabbed from the Depot Island Visitor Center. As a large way station on I-95 south, it had a lot to offer the Disney-bound vacationer. On the brochure in his hand, there was a murky picture of a huge ship looming in a smoky indoor ocean. "It's wicked dark in there," said Miles. "Really . . . foggy. Then, of course, there's the pirates. They're just crazy. So—" he scanned the brochure for the right word—"*Authentic.*"

"Miles," said his mother. "Sweetie?"

He froze. "Yes, ma'am?" She was onto him, he knew it. Next she'd ask to speak to his dad, and it'd be all over. Why this? Why him? He should not have been the one left holding this particular bag. Didn't he have enough to worry about, with starting junior high in a few weeks? He ran his tongue along his teeth, wishing he had a cyanide capsule: Mission aborted.

"Miles," she said, "please don't forget how to talk to me." She gave a huge, wet snuffle.

He let out a big breath: She was just drunk, being weepy. "Oh, Mom." Miles felt weepy himself. He could almost smell his pillow back home. He could have it back right now, have her back. But he couldn't narc on his father's mistake. That was Carrie's word for it: Narc-ing. Dad was coming back, Carrie had said. How would it look if his children weren't where he'd left them?

"No, really," said Mrs. LaPine. "I mean, Carrie: I love that girl, but your sister talks to me like I'm holding a drug-sniffing dog. And your father, even before the split—well."

"Yes, well," said Miles. If he agreed instantly, there was a chance she wouldn't go on.

"I'm sorry, Miles, I shouldn't speak poorly of your dad. I think he's turning himself around, I really do." The air horn of a semi blasted outside Miles' window at the Waldorf Motel. He clamped a hand over the mouthpiece of the phone. When he put the receiver back to his ear, his mother was saying, "—wouldn't have let you kids go with him if I didn't think he could handle the responsible. The responsive. What? The responsbibility, Jesus."

There was no one around to see her like this, but Miles' face reddened for her all the same. He could almost see the tall green bottles on their counter, crowding out the toaster oven. The labels had pictures of swans on them, or maybe rabbits.

"Of course, I was half-hoping he'd fuck it all up and I'd get to rush in and save you kids," said his mother. "Ha-ha!"

"Well! This is going to be some phone bill!" said Miles. Since the divorce, the quickest way out of any conversation was by mentioning money. Carrie had taught him that.

His mother yawned in his ear. "All right, little you, get some sleep.

I love you more than breathing. Say hi to your sister and father for me. Hell, you can even give them both hugs." She snuffled in the phone again. "Pricks."

Miles hung up just as another truck horn tore the air outside. He pulled aside the plastic blind and looked out across Depot Island. Semis and tankers (after seven days, Miles now knew the difference) crept past each other like caterpillars in the white lamplight. Depot Island wasn't really an island at all, but a flat, round mini-town devoted to diesel and comfort, a plate of wide roadways and low concrete buildings. The whole thing was ringed by tall pines, which did give the impression that if you went beyond those trees, you'd fall into some magically conjured water, or perhaps off the Earth itself. Every night, hundreds of streetlights clicked on together and made fake yellow daylight until the real thing came again. Somewhere out there in the never-night was Carrie, though she was most certainly not alone. She was a person who made friends easily, as long as you weren't related to her.

Somewhere even more out there, beyond the pine barrier, was their father. And strung between them, in an ever-thinning strand, were the questions: Was he still driving the blue Datsun they'd arrived in a week earlier? Or was he stuck somewhere with no way to call them? Was he okay? Was he scared? Miles might have known more, except Carrie wouldn't let him read the blue notepaper their dad had left for them, along with some money. She kept it folded in the pocket of the tight jeans Miles had thought their mother had forbidden Carrie from wearing. All Carrie would say about the note was that their father was on an important mission. Miles could understand that, couldn't he?

This past year and a half had not been his father's best. Dennis LaPine had been caught having an affair with the principal at the high school where he taught, getting the two of them fired in the process. Then, during the divorce from Miles' mother, it'd come to light that he'd also had a relationship with Miles' sixth-grade teacher, Miss Hansberry. After all that ugliness, this trip from Massachusetts to Orlando was supposed to be a healing, of sorts, the first spoonful of dirt back into a hole of Dennis LaPine's own digging. They'd stopped here at Depot Island at the end of Day One. In the morning, when Miles had wakened to find his father gone, Carrie said he'd gone out. It wasn't until 11:00 that night, when Miles was crying and trying to dial the police on the motel-room phone, that Carrie had showed him the folded-up piece of notepaper and told him their dad would be back in a few days, and in the meantime to please grow the fuck up. Anyway, she said, he'd left them some just-in-case money.

It was past midnight now, and Miles was alone at the Hi-Ho Diner. Carrie was late for dinner again. She'd been showing up a little later each night. Miles had bought his daily pair of Slim Jims that morning and had finished the last inch of them at ten, just before calling their mother. Arlette, the overnight waitress, cruised by his seat at the counter. Then she backed up, slowly, making beeping noises, like a truck. This had become their thing that week, Miles looking sad and Arlette cheering him up. She didn't know about his father. Miles was always sure to make some mention of him: He was sleeping back at the room, he was over at the video arcade. (These were Carrie's suggestions. "Do you want the cops involved?" she'd said. "Do you want Dad to go to jail just because he's taking care of stuff?") But like everyone Miles had come across at Depot Island, Arlette didn't seem overly concerned about the twelve-year-old boy wandering around for days on end.

Arlette looked at the clock. "What is that girl's problem?" she said. "You know, I think you ought to just order the Big Haul tonight and stick her with the check."

Arlette was a tall, big-hipped woman in a stained yellow waitress dress that was at least a size too small. She had pomegranate lips and tall hair the color of the copper colander back at Miles' house. Arlette powdered her face so that it was two shades whiter than the backs of her hands. Miles wanted to marry her, or at least get a job where he could watch her walk back and forth for hours. He knew she'd miss him after his father came back to correct his mistake.

Carrie showed up near 12:30 and sat down two stools over from Miles. She smelled like cigarettes, diesel, and beer. If you took away the diesel, Miles thought, it would smell pretty good. But everything on Depot Island smelled like diesel.

"Hey, large and in charge," she said. "Call Mom?" Miles nodded. "Say anything stupid? No? Good. Any word from D-A-D?" Miles shook his head. "Heard a good one today," Carrie said. "How do you keep a homo in suspense?"

"How?" said Miles. When she didn't answer, he said, "How?" again.

"Exactly," she said. This was what she called taking care of her little brother.

Carrie was wearing cutoffs and a black Lynyrd Skynyrd t-shirt.

When she'd left the room that morning, she'd had on a brown tank-top. "Where'd you get the new shirt?" Miles said.

"From Dallas," she sighed. She made a secret smile and began crossing and uncrossing her legs on her high stool. Dallas was her new Depot Island boyfriend. She'd met him their second night there, at the big video arcade on the south side of the Island. She'd taken Miles there to cheer him up. Nights were the worst for Miles; weren't nights when all the separate parts of a household were supposed to fold back together, keeping each other snug and safe?

This guy Dallas worked at one of the repair centers, draining truck oil all day. He'd joined Miles and Carrie for dinner the other night. Arlette had been especially un-nice to Dallas, which made Miles like her even more. But Dallas was Carrie's dream guy. He looked to be a few years older than Carrie, which was just about the right age for her. She hadn't gone with a guy her own age since she was eleven. Dallas had a scraggly brown mustache and a wide leather bracelet, and he kept calling Miles "man," as in: *What grade you in, man?* And: *Your sister's really eighteen, right, man?* Still, Miles couldn't hate him all the way: Dallas had invited Miles along to go see the Fourth of July fireworks with Carrie and him.

"So, Dallas gave you a t-shirt, huh?" Miles said to Carrie. "You guys gonna get *married* now?" He was teasing, but Carrie seemed to genuinely consider the question.

She shrugged. "Or we might just shack up."

This was how you survived at Depot Island, according to Carrie's plan: Eat small bits of food every few hours; wash it down with free water from restrooms. Dinner can be pancakes or French toast, sometimes eggs, whatever's under three dollars. If you get too hungry, go back to the Waldorf and take a nap. But not if there's a bandana on the door-knob. Carrie had figured that if they each used five dollars a day, they could make the money last till their father got back. Now, at day seven, she was thinking they should probably make it two-fifty a day each.

Miles allowed himself two video games a day at the arcade. (Carrie liked to brag that she got all her games for free, but then Miles didn't have a Dallas to slouch along behind him with a pocket full of quarters.) Sometimes a trucker would pull over and ask Miles to go into the Hi-Ho for cigarettes from the machine. Miles would usually get fifty cents for his trouble. One time, when Miles thanked one of them, the guy said, "Oh, I can be a lot more generous than that." Miles didn't like the way the trucker looked at him, and he ran off before the guy could say anything more. Now, though, he was wondering what the guy had meant. Maybe he needed someone to run across the Island for something? Miles could do that. He hated the thought of having to choose between food and video games.

They couldn't go on like this forever. Or could they? There were good points to their situation: In his seven days at Depot Island, Miles had showered only once. He still hadn't opened the new toothbrush his mother had tucked in his luggage. Sometimes, even with the shadows of trucks creeping across the walls and ceiling at night, Miles felt *good*. He felt like he might return to school a new man: Tough, traveled; despite Carrie's comments, he felt thinner. It would be nice not to come back as himself.

"Can you see, man?" said Dallas. It was the next night, Fourth of July. They were standing in the bed of Dallas' big blue pickup truck, waiting for the fireworks to begin. Carrie was sitting on the wheel well, mouthing a cigarette and trying not to squint in the smoke. She'd changed into her tight white jeans for the occasion. Miles had thought the fireworks would be their chance to get away from the Island, if only for an evening, see something that wasn't perfectly flat and day-lit at night. He'd thought wrong. Someone had actually herded all the tractor-trailers out from the main sleeping lot behind Denny's, and in their place allowed hundreds of people to park and watch. These were people from the little towns around Depot Island, Dallas informed him, places too poor to put on fireworks of their own.

The vehicles were jammed in a semicircle, a harbor of pickup trucks fanning out from where some men were leaning long metal tubes against wooden sawhorses. Miles guessed these were the launchers. One of the men seemed to be having trouble standing; at one point he leaned over and vomited. Miles realized all the guys were swigging from tall cans and leaning sloppily on the equipment. He thought back to the fireworks displays he'd seen at home, rigidly controlled events where you weren't allowed within a hundred feet of the launching area.

"Shouldn't the fire department be here?" Miles asked.

Dallas nodded toward the guys holding the beers. "That *is* the fire department."

Ten minutes later the sky was flashing and the air was cracking. The sawhorses, it turned out, didn't make for great stands; the mortar tubes were aimed so low that the crowd had to lean backwards to see the fireworks exploding over the diners and fueling stations behind them. Nonetheless, the crowd ooh-ed and yay-ed at the display. Dallas handed Miles a beer as if he'd just asked for one. Miles looked at Carrie. She made a worried face—a mother's face—then closed her eyes and took a gulp from her own can. Miles brought his to his lips, but didn't tip it far enough for the beer to enter him. The smell, though: Home, the way it used to be, when everything was regular.

His father would come in late, always late—so many department meetings and softball games—and he'd stop by Miles' room to kiss his son's head. Miles would pretend he was asleep, and sometimes his father would linger inches from his face, breathing his warm, bready booze-air, as if he wanted to tell Miles something. Miles always wished his father was not a teacher, but a secret agent, and in those moments at his bedside, it would seem true. Called to some dangerous mission in Iran or Russia, he'd come to kiss his only son not goodnight, but goodbye. Take care of everyone, son; you're the man of the house now.

After a minute, Miles' father would stand up and turn away. Then he'd trip over some toy or book Miles had left on the floor, and he'd go out in a hiss of swear words, leaving the door open and the hall light blazing through the slits of his son's eyes.

Miles suddenly thought to ask Carrie about the series of stops they'd made along the way down here. Their father had pulled over at every other rest stop and used the bathroom. Was that what had happened? Did he have some disease or something, and was he now lying in some nearby hospital bed wondering where his kids were?

He turned to ask about this, but was distracted by the new event: A large-bellied firefighter was out in front of the mortar tubes now, dancing shirtless and spouting beer from his mouth. He looked like a fountain you'd never want to wish at.

"Fuckin' Ray Billings, man," chuckled Dallas. He nudged Miles. "They call him Big Baby. Now you watch." And not a minute later, someone to the right of them hurled a can of beer, yelling, "Sit yer ass down, Big Baby!" The can hit the pavement next to the large fire-fighter and burst into a foamy mess.

"No fair!" yelled Big Baby. "That one was full!" But he grinned and danced faster, his limbs and bosoms waving at different speeds. Behind him, the other firefighters didn't seem to notice anything. They stayed busy, loading and firing mortars past his head and into the low, dark sky. Miles hung his head back and watched the colors explode over the garage where Dallas worked.

Miles glanced at Carrie, who was still crouched on the wheel well. She was looking annoyed at Dallas, who'd clearly been paying too much attention to Miles. Dallas saw her face and waved her off. Miles took a swig of his beer and moved close to Dallas. A moment later, an elbow hit Miles hard, knocking him down. Miles looked up to ask why, but Dallas was busy kissing Carrie. To Miles, they looked like a couple of dogs cleaning each other's faces. It was her elbow that had gotten him, he realized. That arm was now pressed against Dallas' side, the hand shoved all the way into Dallas' front jeans pocket. Miles could see it squirming underneath the denim. Miles felt an erection coming on and looked away, feeling like the very worst kind of pervert. He held his beer can against his pants, trying to do it as nonchalantly as possible, praying the cold would kill the boner. But it was too late: The hard can felt good, and now he had a picture of Arlette slipping her hand into his own pocket. Miles focused on the fireworks, hoping everyone around him was doing the same.

Big Baby kept dancing and taunting, and from all around them came missiles: beer cans, apples, wadded cigarette packs. He dodged nearly everything that was thrown at him, with a speed and grace that surprised Miles. There was a pause in the abuse, and Big Baby gave a deep, elegant bow to the crowd. Then he threw himself to the ground beside the smoking mortars. Miles turned to ask Dallas what was going on, but he wasn't there anymore. Carrie was gone, too. The truck bed was empty. Looking around, Miles realized everyone else around him was crouched down in the beds of their own trucks. Miles, who still had a full erection, was the only one standing.

"You may want to do this, too," said an old man from the next truck. Miles looked back at the line of cannons. The firefighters were grinning and waving at him. Miles had his hand up to wave back when he realized the mortars were no longer pointed toward the sky. In fact, Miles could see only the holes at the ends of their barrels.

Then he saw nothing, just a white light that grew in a blink and swallowed him up.

He was on his back. There were heavy footsteps on the steel truck bed, and then someone was slapping Miles all over his head. He didn't know what he'd done wrong, what Depot Island fireworks custom he'd violated. Was it his boner? "Sorry!" he yelled. "I'm sorry!"

When the slapping stopped and Miles opened his eyes, the old man from the next truck was standing over him. He shook his head, smiling. "You were on fire a smidge just now," he said, and he showed Miles his palms, which were black. Little bits of burnt fluff floated in the air between them. There was a smell like ruined butter. Miles realized both the fluff and the smell was his hair. He put his hand to his head and it came back patched with blood. He sat up, expecting to see the people around him staring in horror and concern at the boy who'd been hit with fireworks. Instead, everyone was laughing. Not awkward, what-just-happened? laughter, but the good-time laughter of people who now had a story to tell at breakfast tomorrow. What was this world Miles had now spent twelve years in? The old man patted Miles on the shoulder sweetly, and somehow it made him feel even smaller and dumber than the laughter had.

"Where's your mama at?" the old man said. Miles began to invent an answer, and then he was crying so much he could barely form words.

"Buddy, can we bring you somewheres?" said the man.

Miles tried to think of what he was supposed to do. He wasn't supposed to narc, he knew that, he was supposed to name a place that wouldn't lead to more questions. But he was tired of lying, pretending, surviving. "I want my mom," he said.

When Miles called his mother from the Hi-Ho and told her everything, she didn't yell, didn't cry, didn't sound surprised. She just said, "Come home." Then Arlette got on the phone. She shoved Miles away toward the lunch counter and spoke in a low voice to Mrs. LaPine. When she hung up, she walked back over to Miles. "She's gonna wire some money to the Western Union over by the Sleep-Eeze Motel," said Arlette. "Give her a couple hours. Then I'll drive you and your sister to the bus station in Redville."

Miles went back to their room at the Waldorf Motel. No bandana on the doorknob, so he went in. In the daylight, with clothes and bags and Carrie's hair implements everywhere, the room always looked to Miles what he imagined a college dorm room, or an adult apartment, to be like. It had made him feel grown-up, proud. In the light from the fluorescent ring on the ceiling, though, it looked like someone else's room, or a murder scene. Miles stepped across the floor gingerly. He was spooked.

Carrie's white jeans, the ones she'd worn to the fireworks, were twisted like a denim tornado on the end of her bed.

"Hello?" Miles called toward the darkened bathroom. No one answered.

The fear gripped him like a huge, cold fist. He realized, for the first time all week, that if someone were to take him, or kill him, no one here would know or care. He backed out of the room. He would go to the Hi-Ho and wait out the hours there. Nowhere else on Depot Island felt safe. Maybe Arlette would drive him over to the Western Union. He was at the doorway when he looked again at the white jeans on Carrie's bed. They'd been taken off in a hurry.

She had left behind nineteen dollars and eighty-three cents in her pocket. It was wrapped in a piece of blue notepaper.

Carrie, it said,

Change in plans! Okay, so your crazy Dad has fucked up again. I've confirmed, through my many payphone calls along our journey, that an old friend is living not far from here. (Why am I euphemizing? It's Miles' teacher, Ms. Hansberry. I knew her as Joan.) I'm going to see her and seek forgiveness for past sins. I know this was supposed to be our big cool trip together, but I can't move forward with my life until I reconcile some things with this woman. Affairs of the heart and all that. I know YOU will understand. Try and explain it to Miles in a way that he will, too. There's $200 in cashola here. Get your asses on the first bus out of here and see if you can convince your mom not to press charges. I wouldn't trust Miles with anyone but you, kiddo. See you on the flip side, as they say.
Love,
Dad

Miles read the note, and then he read it again. These were words, in English, but he couldn't make them make sense. He read it a third time, wiped his eyes, and then jammed the note and the last of the money in his own pocket.

He left everything else behind in the room and went back to the Hi-Ho.

"One Big Haul," he told Arlette. She raised a painted eyebrow at him. At four dollars, it was the most expensive breakfast on the menu. Miles pulled out his new money and slid a five across the counter to her.

Arlette looked at the bill, then put it in the pocket of her apron. "You went to Western Union already?"

"Nope. Can you swing over there on our way to the bus station?"

"I can. Your sister knows to meet us here?"

Miles took a sip of his water. "She's gonna meet me at the bus. Dallas is driving her. Their last moments together." He looked at Arlette to see if she was buying all this. "Affairs of the heart and all that."

Arlette laughed and reached out to ruffle his hair. To her, he knew, he was a cute little kid, the young chubby guy who said funny, adult-like things. With her arm outstretched, Miles could see down her short sleeve. Her arm was so soft and smooth-looking as it disappeared into the hollow of her armpit. He wanted her to squeeze him—not in a dirty way, just clutch him, almost killing him, until it was time to get on the bus that would take him back to his house and his mother. Miles could see the edge of a tan bra-strap, and he looked away. Okay, now he wanted Arlette to do other things for him. He also had a creeping feeling it would be difficult to appreciate the little stick-girls in his class from now on.

Arlette took her arm back and smoothed down her sleeves. "Big Haul comes with juice and coffee," she told Miles. "You want two juices?"

Miles shook his head. "I'll take the coffee, if you don't mind."

Arlette smirked, then got a glass carafe and poured coffee into the empty cup in front of Miles.

His deal with himself was this: If Carrie showed up before they left, he'd take her with them. If not, she could find her own way home. Or stay, if that's what she wanted. This was more of a choice than she'd given him, but then he was a nicer person. In the meantime, Miles wanted to just sit at the damn counter, eat his giant damn breakfast, and drink his complimentary damn coffee.

The Book of Right and Wrong

This is the kind of town Black Rock, CT, has become: Besides the landscapers and tree specialists, you can hire a team of guys just to come and pick up all the dog shit from your lawn. When Bobby Benoit grew up here, there was no such thing. Now there are three companies with brightly logoed pickup trucks roaming around town. (One is called Doggy Doods.) Bobby wonders if, given his prison record, he could get hired to do even this job.

It's after-school time on the preschool playground, the best and worst hour of Bobby's day. On this sunny April afternoon, he sits at the front of the picnic table by the preschool building, reading the *Black Rock Gazetteer*. His four-year-old son, Cyrus, runs around playing some kind of imaginary baseball game, swatting invisible balls from every angle. As usual, Bobby is the only dad on the playground.

The town paper is full of announcements about committees and zoning regulations, disagreements over moving the YMCA. Black Rock wasn't always this businesslike. In Bobby's day, a high schooler could make extra money dealing pot to his football teammates, and later to the guys he worked with on building sites. Then people started moving up from the city, bringing along serious incomes. Bobby got caught the very first time he sold coke to someone who wasn't born in Black Rock.

The guy, a hedge-fund manager, got off with an $800 fine. Bobby, who was married and had a new baby, went away for four years. When he came home, it was to a town where the streets and addresses were still the same, but the houses had all changed.

Cyrus comes jogging up to the picnic table. He rests a hand on the corner while panting dramatically. His long bangs stick to his forehead. He's already much shorter than the other kids in his class, and the long hair somehow makes him look smaller.

"Whatcha doing?" says Bobby.

Cyrus glares at him, pissed at the interruption. Cyrus will occasionally speak to Bobby in public, and not at all at home. At home, the four-year-old speaks only to his grandmother. Father and son are still getting to know each other. "Killing zombies."

And here Bobby had thought baseball. Instead, his son has been swinging an invisible machete, beheading the children of Black Rock. That'll do a lot for their image around here.

"Dude," says Bobby. "How about something where you play with the other kids? Like tag."

Cyrus looks at him, then runs off again, leaving Bobby to sit there feeling stupid. He will probably do this again—risk the lash—just as he keeps packing a peanut butter sandwich for Cyrus every day even though every lunchbox comes back bearing the same pleading note: Their classroom is next door to the nut-free classroom, says the teacher, and she doesn't want to take any chances. But one of the few things Bobby knows about his son is that Cyrus loves peanut butter. The sandwiches will continue.

There are three picnic tables on the sandy playground. Two are filled with moms, cramming in their adult conversation for the day; at the other table is a pair of Serbian nannies and Bobby Benoit.

A woman walks up: Miranda Lees, a mother he's noticed since September but never spoken to. Looking past her, Bobby sees the women at her picnic table doing a poor job of not watching the two of them. He wonders who dared Miranda to go talk to the big ex-con. "Mr. Benoit?" she says. She pronounces it in the proper French, like Ben-wah.

"It's Ben-oyt."

"Word has it you did some work on the school's wireless network."

"Little bit, yeah." What happened was this: The school director asked if Bobby knew anything about computer networks. Bobby said yes. What he didn't say was where he'd learned it.

"Do you think you could come by and look at our setup?" says

Miranda. "It's not working, and Jason can't be bothered to look at it himself."

He feels bludgeoned by this tumble of words. What setup where? And who is Jason and why is he being such a dick? Bobby glances up at Miranda, grateful for his sunglasses as he takes in her long neck, her tanned shoulders, her toned arms. She is a person who wears workout gear nearly every day—tight Lycra pants or shorts, thin tank tops. In his own sweatpants and t-shirt, Bobby feels, somehow, underdressed.

"What say you, good sir?" says Miranda. "Help a gal out? I'll pay in cash."

"I'm your guy," says Bobby.

At home, the afternoon routine begins. Bobby makes himself a sandwich at the counter while his mother complains about Black Rock and Cyrus silently plays with action figures at the table.

"They passed that new zoning law," says Mrs. Benoit.

"Yeah?" Bobby saw this in the paper, but couldn't be bothered to read past the headline.

"Yeah. Now if you want a shed that's any bigger than an outhouse, you have to have X amount of space between your house and the shed. Oh, but get this: It also can't be right up against a fence or anywhere on the edge of the property line."

"Isn't that kind of where a shed goes?"

"That's what I say!"

"So we couldn't have a shed is what this means?"

"No, *we* could. I just hate when they change the rules for no apparent reason."

He says nothing. If they lived somewhere else, it might be cheaper; but Black Rock has excellent schools and, in Bobby's mother, free childcare. And she might complain, but she'll never leave. And why would she? It's her house, mortgage fully paid off with her dead husband's life-insurance money. Bobby's end is paying for groceries and taxes and miscellaneous expenses—preschool tuition, for instance. For this, he does handyman work: hanging drywall, laying tile, doing light plumbing for people too cheap to shell out for licensed, bonded legitimates. When he doesn't have handyman work, he mows lawns. It's never not a struggle.

Bobby looks at the clock. If he gets over to Miranda's before 3:00, he might return in time to squeeze in a pair of lawn jobs down the street. "Cyrus," says Bobby. The boy leans closer to his Batman and Joker figures, whispering dialogue: *No more will you commit these heinous . . .*

"Hey, Cyrus," Bobby says again.

Bobby's mother steps in. "Your father is speaking." Cyrus looks up at her.

"I gotta go, bud," says Bobby.

"Did you get Mamie's call?" says Mrs. Benoit. "The yard?"

"That's where I'm going, after this first job." He wonders what will happen to his lawn clientele when all his mother's friends die off. Or sell out: Half the neighborhood changed hands last year. With land scarce in Black Rock, people have started buying up older houses and knocking them down to make room for newer, bigger ones. These people don't want some guy with a lawn mower. They want a crew, a truckload of Mexicans rushing in and tag-teaming the landscape, gone in an hour, leaving no trace of themselves.

Cyrus leans up and whispers something to his grandmother. Bobby heads for the door. Mrs. Benoit calls after him. "Can you pick up some popsicles for the man here?"

That tiny exchange—the little whisper, its loud translation—sums up how it is, this last year between Bobby and Cyrus. How it is to have a piece of you that won't acknowledge you. Bobby feels it swelling and twisting in his chest, like a fairytale beanstalk, or a snake. He turns and looks at his son, this little stranger whom he nonetheless loves so much more than his own skin. "Tell Mr. Cyrus I would pick up a goddamn cement truck if that's what he wanted. Tell him I'd pick up the ocean. Tell him all he has to do is ask."

Cyrus grimaces at his figures, looking quietly mortified. Mrs. Benoit smiles a mother's smile: pain, worry, pity. "I think just popsicles will do."

They are a ship of ghosts, the Benoit family. Everyone moves among the others, slipping through doorways and up stairs with as little motion and wind as possible. When Bobby went away, Cyrus was two months old. Cyrus' mother, Sheila, has been dead since just before Bobby got out. Bobby had known she was bipolar—that one's not exactly a silent disease—but she'd always kept on her meds for the sake of their son. One day, she went to the library by the river and put Cyrus in front of the wooden train set in the children's room. Then she went out, swallowed her entire bottle of Depakote, and threw herself to the icy water.

A bipolar suicide and a fuck-up dad: Some hand, thinks Bobby. As he drives across town to Miranda's house, he wonders what would happen if he were to suddenly jerk the wheel and take on one of the huge oaks that buffer the roadside. His mother's getting old: Would Cyrus get a whole new family? Would he have a chance, then, of starting clean? Bobby puts both hands full on the wheel and tightens his fingers around the hard plastic. Dead men make no money.

Miranda's house is on the edge of town, out toward Weston. Bobby once knew a guy on Miranda's street, but like his own neighborhood, so many of these houses have been flattened and remade vast. He pulls his old Cavalier into Miranda's basketball-court-sized driveway and parks behind her black Volvo SUV-thing. Miranda's daughter, Erin, is playing on the slate walkway with another girl Bobby recognizes from the preschool.

"Hey, guys," says Bobby. The girls merely blink up at him.

Inside, Miranda's on the kitchen phone. She smiles at Bobby and waves a *one-minute!* finger. She's wearing black stretch pants and some kind of pink workout top, a different outfit from earlier. It seems possible that she works out more than once a day. The only hint to her age is her neck, which is slightly ropy in a way you don't see on women in their twenties or thirties. Bobby's neck is more like a block of ham. He's not fat, exactly—he has the well-padded muscle of a one-time high-school football player—but Miranda must look at him and see butter coursing through his veins.

Off her phone call, Miranda offers him some lemonade. "Erin and Cassidy just made it," she says. Bobby pictures kids stirring with their hands. "I'm good," he says.

On the counter is an open planner. Today's page has something scribbled in for every hour. He sees his name written across the 3PM slot: BOBBY B. He likes the sound of that: Bobby B. It's a little friendly, a little more-than-friendly.

The network in question is housed in the basement, a huge finished area with puffy leather couches and heavy brown pots of ceiling-high grasses. The TV hanging on the wall is bigger than Bobby's windshield. Looking for the network room, Bobby heads for the door beside the TV.

"Whoops!" says Miranda. "Nanny's quarters."

"Of course," says Bobby.

"Not that there's a nanny!" she says quickly. "I use a babysitter three nights a week, but that's it." He wonders if she tells this to everyone, or if he just makes her feel uncomfortably wealthy.

Miranda leads him to another door on the other side of the couches. Inside are two metal racks of equipment. Bobby counts three TiVos, a digital music server, various amplifiers, assorted routers, and a pair of high-end Apple computers. The racks are on casters, for easy access. Bobby had imagined he'd be working on a regular computer network, not a media system. The room hums like a nest of sleeping robots.

"Wow," says Bobby. "Where's the failsafe button?"

He worries he's just been lippy, as is his habit, but the remark brings an unexpected smirk to Miranda's face. "Jason likes to have complete control over the household media," she says. She takes a long breath and suddenly there's something unfinished about the sentence, some thought hanging back on her tongue. Bobby begins imagining what her naked back might look like.

She's still talking: ". . . TiVo-ing every soccer game, every Lacrosse match. . . ."

He pictures sweat sparkling between her shoulder blades; her back arched slightly, spine like a string of pearls sunk just beneath a sandy ocean floor.

Miranda's hand appears on his arm. He flinches, and it's gone. Immediately, he wants it back on him.

"I'm sorry," she says. "Is it wrong that I'm asking about it?"

"What?" She'd changed subjects while he was making dirty little movies.

"Your time inside."

Wow, he thinks: from TiVo to prison in under a minute. His own mother hasn't even asked about his "time inside." Amazingly, he hears himself tell Miranda, "Go ahead."

"Was it scary?" says Miranda. There's a light in her eyes he hasn't seen before.

"Was it scary," he repeats, watching that light dance and flicker. "Yes, sure, sometimes. Mostly it was kinda boring." Her eyes are dim again, and suddenly he wishes he had a scar to show her. "Well, this one time I watched a Hispanic dude stab a guard in the lunch room. Toothbrush handle to the neck. Blood everywhere."

"Really?" And there's that flicker again.

"Sure." The attack in question had actually happened a week before his arrival, but she doesn't need to know that.

Upstairs, someone screams. Bobby and Miranda look at the ceiling. Bobby thinks: Goddammit, Cyrus. Then he remembers Cyrus isn't here. Miranda runs up the stairs.

Bobby looks around. Should he run up, too, or just get to work? He's unsure of his role here—is he a fellow parent or the handyman? He glances into the network room, which only hums at him unhelpfully. He bounds upstairs after Miranda.

She's in the kitchen, her back to the basement door. Little Erin sits on the counter, wailing away into her mother's chest, gangly limbs wrapped around Miranda's neck and ribs.

"What happened" says Bobby.

"Sshh!" hisses Miranda.

The other little girl, Cassidy, is there. Her fingers are filthy. "I pretended some dirt was peanut butter."

"Oh," says Bobby. "And she ate it and it was gross, huh?"

Miranda turns partway to him. "No, she's violently *allergic* to peanuts, and Cassidy there was using that information to scare the shit out of my daughter." She glares at Cassidy.

"She said she was gonna put it on me," Erin wails. She pauses to sneer at the other girl before burying her face into her mother's bare shoulder.

Cassidy shrugs. "I thought it was funny."

"Yeah, well, we'll see how funny it is when your mother gets here," says Miranda.

Erin forces out a sob.

"Hey," says Bobby, crouching down by Cassidy. "How about we go outside and wait for your mom?" He doesn't know if, or how, the girl's mother has been called already. Mainly he just wants to get the fuck out of the kitchen.

Cassidy looks at him, then away. "I'm not a'pposed to talk to you."

"Oh, sure. No talking to strange men, right? I gotcha."

"No, just to *you*. Miranda told us not to talk to you."

Bobby can feel Miranda's eyes on his back now. He stays in midcrouch, frozen, looking past little Cassidy. If he stays, he might as well be telling Miranda to go ahead and treat him like a slave. He could say screw the gig, just walk out the door. Finally, he stands and heads for the basement stairs. Over at his house, they could use the cash.

At home that night, Bobby finds his mother at the kitchen table, going through a cardboard banker's box. Their kitchen, which he's seen now for thirty-seven years, has never looked so dark. Over at Miranda's the cabinets were light, lovely wood, the color of butter. Mrs. Benoit's cabinets are the color of pine bark. What little light gets thrown by the chandelier over the table gets swallowed up by all this dark wood.

Bobby makes a bowl of Corn Pops, grabs a Budweiser, and sits down at the table. "Cyrus found this stuff," Mrs. Benoit says. "We were cleaning the attic."

She's got a jumble of papers in there, all colors and shapes; here and there, pipe cleaners and straws stick out like arms and legs trapped under rubble. All too familiar, this box. It's the third time he's seen it in the past year. "Cyrus found this," Bobby says.

"Yup," she answers, but she won't look at him. She keeps it in her closet, he knows, for trotting out whenever she wants Bobby and Cyrus to realize how similar they really are, how they need to build a bridge across the missing years.

"Look at this," she says. "You remember this?" She reaches in and plucks out a little booklet of folded-over paper. "I asked Cyrus what was bothering him, and he said he was worried he wouldn't be smart enough for kindergarten. Him—can you imagine? So I showed him this." She pushes the booklet across the table to her son. In ugly block letters, it says THE BOOK OF RIGHT AND WRONG. Inside, each of the pages has one line of huge, leany kid-printing:

There was a man and he fell asleep in spectacular dirt.
When he woke up God said Write a book.
So he did and it was called The Book of Right and Wrong.
Everyone loved him and he was the smartest man in the world.
Everyone still knows his name!
The End.

The back cover is a drawing of a man with balloon-like arms and legs. Brown splotches blot his face and hands—the dirt he'd slept in. He is smiling and waving at the reader. Bobby has a vague memory of writing this in preschool, the day after a Sunday school argument about who might have written the Bible. It was the first and last time he ever got anything out of church.

"He's so nervous about September," says Mrs. Benoit. "These next four months are going to be excruciating for him."

"And you were hoping to inspire him by my example?" Bobby says.

She points a finger at him. "You had the stuff. This was very advanced for a four-year-old. What kid that age knows how to write 'spectacular'?"

"I didn't even know what it meant," Bobby says, but even he has to smile at the word.

"Well, when your preschool teachers saw this, they wanted me to petition to get you skipped right to first grade."

"Then I'm glad you fought them on it." He's still smiling, but no longer in such a nice way.

"It's what I thought best at the time. I didn't think you were ready for the pressure."

Good thing I was kept sheltered from pressure, thinks Bobby. He gets up from the table, scraping his beer bottle along with him. "Well, you always used to say you hoped I had one just like me one day." She used to scream it, actually, when he was sixteen. "Maybe your wish came true, Ma."

The next afternoon, Bobby sits at the front of the playground picnic table. Miranda slides in next to him. Behind his sunglasses, he closes his eyes. She smells like lemons.

"I am so sorry," she says. "I *never* told Cassidy and Erin not to talk to you."

"Whatever. *I* would."

"No, see, stop. What I said was, 'Don't bother Mr. Ben-wah.' Sorry— Ben-oyt. Because you'd be working, and they'd be crawling all around asking questions. The system works perfectly now, thank you." She pats his hand.

She looks off toward the far corner of the playground, so Bobby helps himself to a good, long gawk at her small, pretty breasts, which nestle—not bulge—inside her ribbed tank top.

Miranda turns back to him. "Erin lives in terror of having another allergic reaction," she says. "It's crazy, I know, and I'm sure I sound like one of those allergy moms." She waves her fingers at the other picnic table, her usual group of women. "But you'd understand if you'd ever seen your kid writhing on the floor with her face swelling up."

"I'll bet." Instinctively—it *is* instinct now, he realizes—he looks for his own son. Cyrus is by the front fence, holding a stick. He's up on tiptoes, trying to knock a bee out of the air.

"Oh, plus," says Miranda, "something like that happens, guess who gets blamed? 'Well, it was on *your* watch, Miranda.'"

Bobby doesn't say anything. He doesn't seem to be part of this conversation. Then her hand appears on his arm again.

"Why didn't we have all this when we were kids?" she says. "All this allergy stuff, peanuts and gluten and whatnot."

"Aw, we were protected," he says. "All that asbestos and lead paint kept our bodies shielded from the glutens."

She laughs. "Jason says it's because our diets have gotten so refined. We're so removed from true nature, he says, that our kids are literally weaker than we were. He says we're going to civilize ourselves into extinction."

Bobby pictures Jason, or who he imagines Jason to be—long chin, slender hands, neatened eyebrows—in post-apocalyptic rags, trying to subdue a wild boar with his last remaining TiVo.

"Hey," Miranda says. "Do you get a lot of work?"

He leans back and looks at her. "It's seasonal," he says. "People typically need more help with their technology in the spring and fall." Which might be true. Mainly, he'll say anything to avoid mentioning his lawn work. Suddenly it seems very important that she not know about his lawn work.

"I used to do print layout," Miranda says. She rolls her eyes. "In my old life. Pre-*here,* I mean. What if I made business cards for you?"

Miranda's business cards make a little magic. Bobby gets a half-dozen new clients within a week, and eight more over the next week. They're all quickie jobs, but that's the name of the game, according to Miranda: volume. Become known as reliable, a fixer of people's stuff, and soon, says Miranda, you're indispensable. This sounds good to Bobby. He pictures himself getting to the point where he's a real company, maybe with a logoed pickup truck of his own, like the dog-shit guys. He'll hire someone to keep his books. The accountant will say, "The books look good this month, Mr. Benoit. Why don't you take a vacation?" He pictures his mother, Cyrus, and himself standing on the deck of a big, white cruise ship.

Miranda herself takes up a good part of his schedule. Since that first job in her basement, he's been at her house almost daily, doing everything from helping her hang clusters of family photos to setting up an invisible fence for the new dog that's arriving any day now from the breeder. Miranda makes him sit down for coffee before getting to work, and as she prepares their drinks he always finds himself lingering on those shoulders, tan and exposed. Bobby has yet to see Mr. Miranda, who does something financial in New York.

The third week in, Bobby stops mowing his mother's friends' lawns.
His days, outside of Cyrus' school schedule, are filled with appoint-
ments for school moms, or friends of school moms. The cards Miranda
made for him say:

WIFE SUPPORT
Robert M. Benoit
Fixing Everything Your Husband Can't
(or Won't!)

At the bottom corners, there are little tools: a hand-saw in one,
a crescent wrench in the other. Frankly, they make him cringe. The
layout is nice, but Wife Support? It makes him sound like a gay best
friend. Worse, it pits him against the husbands, who are not likely to let
such a thing pass. He remembers the preschool auction, back in Feb-
ruary, when these guys were whipping out their checkbooks to outbid
each other on their kids' classroom artwork. One guy at Bobby's table
paid $1,200 for a mirror decorated around its borders with glued-on
bottle caps. Bobby later saw the same mirror, minus the bottle caps, at
Target for $40.

His clients have strikingly similar setups: media room, networked
TiVos, house wired for sound in every room—and a husband who
had some bat-shit system installed and didn't explain any of it. Often,
it's something simple—a universal remote that just needs its codes
reset, or a wireless router needing a quickie firmware upgrade. Bobby
becomes proficient with all sorts of things he could never have in his
own house.

Sometimes it's too simple to possibly be true. One time Bobby finds
a server unplugged at both ends, the power cord lying coiled, neatly,
on the carpet in a roomful of blind, humming witnesses. It reminds
him of the little rope piece from the game Clue. Was it Mrs. Peacock in
the library with the power cord? Or was it Colonel Mustard spending
all his time in the city?

On the playground, Bobby is no longer the husky interloper. He's
welcomed into the picnic-table conversation, greeted at the door,
smiled at. Sometimes the ladies touch him on his shoulder. When
Bobby ditches his sweats-and-t-shirt outfit for a decent pair of jeans and
a button-down, they fuss over him like he's a handsome new exchange
student at their high school. Or, more realistically, the slow kid on
picture day: It's condescending, but he'll take what he can get. He

thinks of them, late at night, faces and bodies flashing by as if reeling through a slide carousel.

Sometimes, as he's drifting off, he imagines a showdown with Miranda's husband. The fantasy is: They're at the school auction night. Bobby's dressed up; Miranda looks amazing. Miranda spends her whole night talking to Bobby. The husband gets pissed and pulls on Miranda's arm. Bobby steps in. The husband looks him up and down and says, "Who let *you* in here?" Bobby breaks his face with one shot. Bobby and Miranda ride off—in her car. Later, she and Erin are on the deck of the big, white cruise ship with Bobby and Cyrus. The sun is sinking into the water's edge and it's almost time to go down for the buffet. Lying on the twin bed in his old room, Bobby plays this one over and over.

One afternoon in May, Bobby and Miranda are in her kitchen. School is ending in a few weeks. Outside, Cyrus and Erin play like old pals on the giant wooden climbing structure in Miranda's backyard. As Bobby's been brought into the playground fold, so has Cyrus—and magically, no more killing, no more zombie-talk. As a rule, he still doesn't speak directly to Bobby, but that's okay. He's a happier kid, and this is enough for Bobby.

"Got a good one for you today," says Miranda. They're drinking iced coffee at the tall, granite-topped prep island. She pulls the straw from her cup and chews on the bottom end. "Speaker in the big bathroom is out."

"Which one?"

"What, which speaker?"

"No," says Bobby. "Which big bathroom? Your bathrooms are all the size of tennis courts."

She grins and pokes at him with her straw. "Funny."

Following Miranda up the stairs, Bobby's hands are moist: He's never done speakers before, or any kind of in-wall wiring. This is where he gets found out. Even though she knows he's not an electrician or audio expert, she's come to think of him as reliable Mr. Fixit. Once that wall behind the speaker is opened up, Mr. Fixit will vanish, leaving in his place Mr. Sort-of-Competent. And who wants to hire that guy?

It's in the master bath. Great, thinks Bobby: something the man of the house sees every day. If Miranda doesn't catch Bobby's mistake, whatever that turns out to be, Mr. Miranda certainly will. In the bathroom, there are two speakers, compact white Boses perched in the upper corners like little white owls. The whole bath is huge—double shower encased in glass, six-foot countertop with two basins, electronic toilet. Bobby can't imagine shitting in this room. It would feel wrong, like crapping in the middle of a museum, or a bank.

Miranda uses the universal remote to turn on the sound system. Music funnels out of the far speaker. The one above the toilet crackles.

"Bad cable," Bobby says. That's in-wall stuff. Here comes the sweat down the back.

"You like Billy Joel?" says Miranda, nodding at the working speaker.

"Not really."

She laughs. "What, you think it's old music? Is that it?"

"More like preparing-to-be-old music. Like Sting, or Bonnie Raitt."

She smiles and gives him the finger.

"You can stand on the toilet if it'll make it easier for you," Miranda says, and he climbs up to look at the speaker. To his left is that enormous countertop, with a wall mirror that runs its entire length. To his right is the window; he can see Cyrus and Erin squirreling up and down the play structure. From way up here, Cyrus seems so normal.

Miranda moves in beside the toilet to supervise. Bobby's stretched up, feeling desperately at the back of the speaker, praying for a loose connection, something that won't require opening up the wall, or dealing with walls in general. At the same time, he is very aware that his shirt has pulled up over his gut.

"What do you think?" Miranda says. He can almost feel her grimacing at his exposed belly. With his free hand, he tugs down the shirt.

"I think you're too young to be listening to such shitty music."

"Ha-ha," she says. "I meant about the speaker. But thank you."

In the mirror over the sinks, he can see her body in profile. Her workout pants, as always, broadcast the buttocks of a twenty-year-old. He can see the dark of her nipples against the thin, white tank top. Bobby feels himself hardening. Then he looks up and sees her, seeing him, in the mirror.

She's not smiling, not turning away, she's just looking at his ridiculous crotch. He forgets to breathe. She tilts her head up at him now, and their eyes meet. "I'm sorry," says Bobby. "You're just such a beautiful—I'm sorry."

He turns his body to climb down, but she puts a hand on his hip. Then, without a word, she reaches up and tugs at the button on his jeans. Bobby still has a hand on the speaker overhead, and he grips it tighter now to keep his balance. If he falls, he'll go through the window behind him and down into the backyard. By the time he manages to take a breath, Miranda has his pants open and the waistband of his underwear down, just a little, so that the tip of him is exposed. Bobby hopes he's not smirking. He's looked at a fair amount of porno in his day, and this is almost a stock scene. He thinks of those letters to dirty magazines: *I always thought these letters were fake, until one day it happened to me. . . .* Miranda glances up at him again, then ducks her head. He feels himself disappear into the warmth of her mouth. His entire body seems to vibrate.

He puts a hand on her head, sliding his fingers into her hair. He closes his eyes, having pictured this act so many times already. "That's right," he whispers.

Later, he still won't know which it was—the hand on her head or the words. But standing there, he doesn't realize it's gone wrong until the cold air swarms the damp head of his penis. Then she's gone and he's left alone in her bathroom, standing on the super-toilet with his pants open. As he climbs down, he glances out the window. Cyrus and Erin are sitting on the top deck of the play structure. Though they're the same age, Cyrus looks like he could be Erin's little brother. They're facing the house, side by side, hands on laps. It looks a little too perfect, a little too we-didn't-see-anything.

He finds Miranda in the kitchen. She's slamming things around in the sink.

Bobby puts a hand on her shoulder. "Listen, I don't think they saw."

She stares at him a moment, eyes and mouth dropping wider, then jerks her head toward the kitchen window. "Oh my God, the *kids?*" she screams. She flings his hand back at him. "You're disgusting," she says. "You're just a. . . ." She gestures at him, but the words don't come. For this he is grateful.

"I should go," he says.

She glares at him. "You think?"

The ride home with Cyrus is quiet, ugly—not unlike a regular ride home from school, before father and son were accepted into society. Bobby is glad Cyrus hadn't started talking to him more even when things got good. He couldn't take it if Cyrus had become chatty and sweet and *then* given him some new silent treatment now that something bad has clearly happened with Erin's mommy. In this way, Cyrus is the reliable one.

* * *

It's the last week of school. Bobby leans against the fence, watching Cyrus run around. Only three days until the year ends. Then it's a long, silent summer before kindergarten. Bobby is nervous: Cyrus is smart, but so is every other kid in Black Rock. In an average town, he'd be a star; but in an average town, you get an average education. Furthermore, when Bobby was this age, he was writing his little books and giving them to all the grownups he knew. Cyrus knows a lot of impressive words, but can't identify half his ABCs.

He glances at Miranda. She's over at the picnic table, chatting with her pals. She and Bobby haven't spoken in the weeks since the incident. It's obvious to Bobby that she's rattled. After all, he's seen something secret: her vulnerability, her loneliness. At night in bed, trying to replay the memory, he can't seem to focus on just the good part, can't slow it down. It's too brief, and it ends so jarringly—like a DVD that suddenly skips to some other, awful scene. Still, in a weird way, it keeps him going: Someone like her wanted him enough to just break down and take him. He wonders how long she'd been resisting. And every night he wonders if she's in her bed across town, going over the moment for herself.

By the playground fence, Bobby checks Cyrus' lunchbox: squashed, empty milk carton; baggie of baby-carrot stubs; half-eaten peanut butter sandwich.

Gretchen Hill comes over. "Do you have time tomorrow? Edward just bought this new thing that will beam your TV signal to a computer anywhere in the world."

Bobby's done one of these. It was a hive of quirks. "So he brought it home and he has no idea how to set it up."

She smiles. "That's why I'm calling in Wife Support."

He pulls out his pocket planner, flips to June. "Can't do tomorrow, but I got time Friday afternoon."

"Done. Thanks, Bobby!"

This is how it's gone lately: business as usual—if anything, busier than usual. He'd been holding his breath, waiting for the Miranda thing to come bite him in the ass. But she seems to have kept her silence, which is a blessing. Just as he's written his last-ever tuition check for preschool, here comes the ugly new tax situation: His mother's taxes are doubling, with July 1 as the first new bend-over date. As long as Bobby keeps getting jobs, and so long as the roof doesn't start leaking or no one has to go to the hospital, he might just be able to make that first check.

On July 1, he'll go to Town Hall, where the tall, hairy-eared guy behind the counter will ask Bobby's address. Then the guy will haul out his huge ledger book, flip it open, and move his finger up and down the pages until he finds *Benoit, Mary A.* The town's tax bills are computer-generated, but when it's time to pay up, they still use a big leather-bound book. It's probably the same book they used when Bobby's father paid his taxes years ago, back when he probably knew what was coming for Black Rock but kept writing a new check every quarter anyway, sticking his family deeper into this town. And like his father, Bobby will hand over his share of everyone else's share. And on October 1, if all goes well, he'll do it again. Because that's how it's done.

Cyrus whips by. He's been getting rough again lately, playing the scary chasing games. Apparently, Miranda's house was his sole source of calm. Now that Bobby knows all these moms, he feels obliged to try and rein in the boy. He's thinking Sunday school might be a good influence. A kid can't start kindergarten acting like an animal.

"Yo, Cy," he calls. The boy stops, gives him a *Yeah?* look. But he doesn't *say* it, embarrassing his father. This is called progress.

"Let's cool it, man," says Bobby. "Stop terrorizing the kids, 'kay?"

Cyrus gives a little nod, then trots off in a mope. He's been Mr. Helpful at home lately, aiding his grandmother with dinner, Windexing her windows. Bobby knows it's because of the money-worry, which courses through the house like electricity. They're in a three-way race for the first ulcer. The past few nights, Bobby's been going in to look at Cyrus, just to watch him sleep. Sleeping Cyrus is the better-world version of Regular Cyrus: No one's ever looked so delicate, no one's face has ever been so smooth and unburdened. Then there'll be a sound like ice being crushed under car wheels, and Bobby will realize his son is grinding his teeth in his sleep.

On the playground, Miranda appears beside Bobby. "Hey, buddy," she says cheerfully.

"Jesus," he says. "Hi." She looks amazing—tanner than usual, in a pink tank top and gray lycra shorts. A skinny white bra strap peeks out from beneath the shoulder of her tank top. Is he the reason she's started wearing a bra?

"Ever work with GPS systems?" she says. She speaks as if they'd just hung out the day before.

"Sure," he lies.

"Great. We just got Erin this cell phone that doubles as a GPS so the parents can know where the child is at all times. You know—because of kindergarten? It's kind of a must-have."

Kindergarten is 8:30 A.M. to noon, the same hours as the preschool.

"Friday, 4:00?" says Bobby. "I got a thing with Gretchen just before that." If Miranda's jealous, she doesn't show it.

"Can you do six?" she says. "Erin has ballet in the afternoon."

Then why the fuck don't you wait till Monday? Bobby wants to say. Maybe *he'd* have plans that late. Maybe *he'd* be eating with his family, or maybe *he'd* even have a date.

"Okay," says Bobby.

"Great! Jason'll be there, too. You'll finally get to meet him!"

Cyrus lopes by, growling at some kid he's chasing. Out of the corner of his eye, he sees Bobby and slows his gait.

"Um. Won't that be awkward? Me meeting your husband?"

Miranda looks at him. "Why would that be awkward?" Bobby starts to answer, but stops: She looks genuinely puzzled.

"No reason at all," he says. "Friday it is." He watches her head back for the picnic table, trying not to stare at the way her shorts cup her behind. Trying. Failing.

If she remembers what happened in her upstairs bathroom, she didn't show it, not now. And for the first time, Bobby sees what kind of person he's been dealing with. For Miranda, their moment was a stupid mistake—something as dumb and everyday as forgetting to pack a snack, or scraping the curb while parallel parking. Nothing to beat yourself up over. What she'd said that day—*You're disgusting*—wasn't even true. Disgusting is something that sticks with you. To her, Bobby isn't even that.

And he'll be there Friday. He can't afford not to.

Cyrus is by the monkey bars. He's paused in mid-chase, holding his hands out like a zombie and lunging for Erin, Miranda's daughter. Erin dodges, laughing. Cyrus notices Bobby, and he puts his hands down. He looks limp, defeated. Good boy, thinks Bobby. Then he thinks again, and beckons to Cyrus.

Cyrus trots over. Bobby takes out his half-eaten sandwich and opens it. The peanut butter glistens on the bread halves like a pair of filthy ponds. "Here," says Bobby, and he grabs Cyrus' wrists together in one hand. Cyrus flinches, but Bobby squeezes hard, pulling the little hands closer. With his free hand, he rubs peanut butter all over his son's palms and fingers. He glances over at Miranda's table. One of her bra straps has escaped from beneath the wider strap of her tank top. It hangs off her shoulder, leaning against her triceps. He wants move in on that piece of shoulder, that tan round between the two straps, and take it in his mouth.

"Why am I doing this?" Cyrus says.

Bobby smiles at him. Whatever the boy's grandmother may say, Cyrus is not as smart as Bobby was at this age. A year from now they may not be able to even live here anymore. Cyrus is Bobby's sole possession, his only contribution to the world. But if he can't be as smart as these Black Rock kids, or as big, or as rich, or as protected, then he can be something they can't. He can be a danger.

Erin runs by. She looks back to see if Cyrus is watching. Bobby holds Cyrus' hands and presses them together until he can hear the peanut butter squelching between the slender fingers. Then he leans against his son's little ear, feeling his lips brush the velvety folds.

"Go get her," he whispers.

Kate the Destroyer

Three years after the fact, it's still what her family's known for around town. A woman lets her unstable ex-husband drive the kids down to Disney World, and only the kids come back? Kate LaPine knows how it looks.

It's ungodly hot, a Friday afternoon in September 1985, and Kate is driving her son Miles in the Datsun. She's bringing him to a fantasy gaming convention at Clark University in Worcester. The event is called something goofy, like GameCon 85. Today's activities are brief: a half-hour orientation, followed by three hours of book signings by authors no normal person would recognize. The rest of the weekend will be given to twelve-hour days of Dungeons & Dragons. *Advanced* Dungeons & Dragons, Miles would say, as if he were a PhD correcting someone at a cocktail party: *That's* Doctor *LaPine to you.*

Strange world he lives in, this boy. Leather sacks of dice, expensive hardcover rule-books, no girls anywhere. It's not shocking, given the departure of his father, that he should keep himself surrounded at all times by older males. And this was once a bearable phase, a little post-divorce fantasyland for a troubled eleven-year-old. But now Miles is fifteen, and still spending all his time, money, and mental energy on it. Isn't it time to start sneaking around, doing drugs? Why can't he be more like his sister?

From the backseat, Miles clears his throat. "This is taking for*ever.*" He's taken to riding back there all the time now. Kate suspects it makes him feel important, as if he's being chauffeured. Out of habit, she glances in the rearview mirror, but the sight of him compels her to look elsewhere. He's in his gaming outfit: hand-sewn tunic, chain-mail vest, long gray cape, sweatpants. Jesus, thinks Kate, he used to be so cute. He was a regular, chubby little boy in his Toughskins and Red Sox t-shirt. Now whenever she sees Miles the Destroyer, it's like walking in on him while he's wearing one of her dresses. Some days, she'd prefer *that.*

"What time am I picking you up?" she says. "Seven?"

"Can't I just take the bus home?"

"I think not, sweetie. Maybe next year." And it's clear now: There will be a next year to this, won't there? He had friends his own age for a time—little gaming buddies. But she's watched them drop off one by one, lured away from the farty, Doritos-rich atmosphere of D&D by the scent of girls, human girls. Kate assumed Miles would follow, too, like that one goose that forgets to shift when the V shifts, but finally races to catch up.

Then, last summer, he started making his own chain mail.

It started with a glove. Not a whole one—he only got as far as the wrist. Fingers were too hard. Then he did a cowl, but the little gaps in the rings kept catching on his eyebrows. Finally, the thing he's wearing now. It's modeled on the sweater vest given him last Christmas by his grandmother. It's not the activity Kate disdains—to see Miles concentrate on anything for more than five minutes, let alone several hours, is amazing. No, the issue is the stuff itself. Chain mail? Even she knows this is boy semaphore for *Hit me.* And of course today he was out there in front of the high school, waiting for her, dressed like this already. He acted like it was the most natural thing in the world, while the kids nearby either pointed and laughed or looked away in embarrassment. Why is it, out of all the things nerdy kids do best, making it harder on themselves is at the top of the list?

Clark University appears up the street on the left, big, brick Jonas Clark Hall standing tall in the middle of everything, like an old man who's wandered into a bad neighborhood. Which is exactly where they are. Kate doesn't like the looks of some of the people on the corner.

"Right here's good," says Miles. He gathers his things together: his forty-pound backpack of guidebooks and dungeon plans, his plastic grocery sack of Mountain Dew and Doritos, his sword.

Kate pulls the car up to a sidewalk teeming with geeks. Heavy men in heavy beards and pit-stained UMass sweatshirts stand arguing with skinny, greasy-haired guys from Worcester Polytech. One or two people are in full battle dress. Miles is only about three-quarters battle-ready, thanks to the sweatpants. For which Kate is strangely grateful: It's as though he's keeping one foot in his actual life, unsatisfying to him as that world might be.

She turns to tell Miles the Destroyer he looks cool, but he's already gone, his door swinging shut. When she sees him again, he's on the sidewalk by the big iron gate, saying his hellos to an odd little collective. There's a middle-aged balding guy with John Lennon glasses; a youngish black man in a wheelchair (metal spikes glint from his wheel-hubs); and a freakishly tall man with hair like a basket of springs. Miles' people.

He turns his head and sees her. For an instant, there's a sweet clarity to his eyes, a familiar rosiness to his chubby cheeks, and she's back at the chain-link fence at the elementary school, watching him line up on the blacktop with the other six-year-olds. Six, the age of *lank*. All those kids, their bodies suddenly catapulted beyond the walls of babyhood, already outgrowing their brand-new fall clothes. Then her son's fifteen-year-old lips recede from their teeth, and Miles the Destroyer silently hurls a word at his mother: *Go!*

She has three-and-a-half hours to do something in Worcester, a dying city whose chamber of commerce recently printed up t-shirts with Eiffel Towers on them and a slogan that said, with no irony, *Worcester: Paris of the Eighties!* What's a single mom to do? thinks Kate. She could go to the museum. She could go to the library. She could go to Elite Billiards and let a dropout from an elite vocational school buy her a soda. Up ahead, she sees the big white sign for Showcase Cinemas.

She picks *Back to the Future.* There are three other movies showing, but this one she's heard of *and* it's the longest one on the bill. The movie is showing in the big theater, the one with the balcony and the huge chandelier. Once upon a time, when Worcester was a real city, this was a real theater—a *theatre*, even. Now, at 3:30 in the afternoon, it looks more like a giant rec-room. When the lights go down, the crowd consists of Kate and maybe a dozen scattered teenagers. They're all huddled into the furthest corners of the place, like basement spiders. People are smoking—and not just cigarettes; she can definitely smell weed—and here and there behind her are the clinking of beer bottles being set down on the painted concrete floor.

The movie starts and the audience, such as it is, seems to be enjoying it. Kate finds it incredibly depressing. The guy playing the teen-aged hero is clearly on the cusp of thirty, and there's a lot of weird Oedipal content Kate could do without.

It would be worth walking out of, if not for the air-conditioning. And for the interesting sounds coming from the balcony above and behind her. These are *guttural* noises, clearly teenaged male, clearly erotic. Then she realizes there's a second voice, also male, but quieter. Someone's double-dating up there. The girls, as always, are practicing the art of discretion, while the boys play it up for the crowd. Ah, memories. Kate only hopes the girls are getting as much out of it. She gets a little flushed thinking about all this. She starts to look back to see what she can see, but shame stops her. These are kids, probably the same ages as her children. She's a grown woman now, a person store clerks frequently refer to as "Ma'am." What if someone she knew were to see her being a pervert?

Finally, curiosity wins out. After all, anyone who would recognize her here, at this time of day, would have some explaining to do themselves. Kate hunches down in her seat, then cranes her neck up and around to see if she can glimpse anything through the balcony railing.

She'd been mistaken about this being a double date. The only figure in the balcony is a tall boy in a white tank top. He's sitting up in his seat, his head tilted back, hands tucked behind his head. He's clearly sleeping, and Kate feels disgusted with herself. How could she have mistaken snoring for sex? This is what it's come to, she thinks: I've begun fabricating other people's sex lives for them.

Then the guy makes that *noise* again, and she instantly recognizes, like a picture coming into focus in a viewfinder, the now unmistakable posture of a teenaged boy receiving a blowjob. He's fairly dark-skinned, and Kate is shocked to realize she's squinting hard for a sign of brown nipples against the white of his shirt. Not half a second later, a dark blur rises from the crotch of the boy in the white tank-top: the head of his date. The blur moves up and down, fixed into a rhythm now. The boy in the chair leans back even further, his seat's old springs creaking under him.

Kate suddenly feels fidgety. She crosses and uncrosses her legs, pretending she's just uncomfortable in her seat, not really willing to consider the alternative explanation. After all, they're in a gross movie theater, the girl probably kneeling in sticky soda and popcorn leavings. Kate's not a prude; you didn't date a guy like her ex-husband if you were a prude. But blowjobs have always felt to her like a fine line between sex and suffocation. If you're lucky, the guy might keep his hands off your head; in Kate's experience, you're not usually that lucky.

The word *lucky* makes her think, improbably, of her lumbering wreck of a son. She would wonder what Miles is doing right now, except that she can picture it already: He's in a bright classroom across town, huddled at a lab table with his fellow non-bathers, rolling dice and fingering little lead figures painted to look like brave, important knights. An epic quest for glory and recognition, to be folded up in a plastic binder at the end of the day.

Miles, she thinks, should be up there in the balcony. Miles should be the one with some dark-haired beauty (or non-beauty, even) going down on him. Kate is startled cold by this thought. The movie right now is Oedipal, sure, but what mother wishes her son were having sex? Then she realizes that, yes, this is true: She wishes Miles were the guy in the white tank-top, experiencing all the joys and pleasures of his youth. Not with his mother rubbernecking from the lower seats, of course.

Things settle down in the balcony after a while, and Kate goes back to watching the crappy movie. By the end, the man-child character has successfully fought off the advances of the girl who would be his mom, and the nerdy character has captured his dream girl. When the lights come up, Kate turns to look for the owner of the white tank-top. But it's different doing this in the light; does she really want to see this person's face? Does she really want to risk making eye contact? Kate rushes for the exit, shame finally winning one today.

Outside the theater it's hot hot hot, and she takes a moment to rest against the cement sidewalk planter before she has to go get in her un-air-conditioned car. Her fellow moviegoers file past her, heading off in different directions. Then, from behind her, someone spits the word *Faggot*.

Kate turns to see a tall Hispanic guy—eighteen? twenty?—shoving a younger kid up against the metal exit door of the movie house. They're a good ten feet away from her. The Hispanic guy has tight, curly hair and a scribbled-looking mustache. His thick chest stretches the shoulder straps of his white Adidas tank-top. His victim is shorter and skinnier, a little dark-haired Whippet of a high schooler in shorts and a plain blue t-shirt. The tall guy leans in and starts hissing threats, dancing the kid's face around with a series of nasty little slaps. Kate gives herself all kinds of reasons for turning away: This could be more complicated than it looks; the younger one may have done something terrible to the other one; she could get shoved into traffic. Then Kate digs her keys out of her purse and starts over to them.

The tall guy sees her approaching. "Keep moving," he says. "This is between me and little cocksucker here."

The younger one has his face down, tucked nearly into his own armpit. "Yeah, just go away, it's okay," he tells Kate. The tall guy twists a handful of the boy's shirt till it's nooselike at his throat. She looks at the boy—*It's okay?* Is he crazy?—and then she realizes: She knows this kid. This is what's-his-name: Jeffrey Tunxis, one of the cool guys from Miles' class. He crapped in Miles' locker freshman year, then denied it in the vice principal's office while his big-boy contractor father snickered away next to him. This kid's been torturing her son since the third grade. If she were him, having Miles LaPine's mother show up at such a moment, she'd rather take the beating, too.

"Let him go," says Kate.

The older kid looks at her, sizing her up. Or picking out her arteries. Does he have a switchblade? She hates herself for thinking this.

"You know what this boy just had in his mouth?" he says.

That's a weird thing to say, she thinks. And then Kate realizes what she's walked in on. The white tank-top, the dark-haired companion: Kate and this pair have been a trio of sorts for the better part of the last two hours. This suddenly *is* a lot more complicated.

"I know you need to let go of him," she says. Her voice sounds so *loud* all of a sudden, as if in an empty room. And of course there's now no one else on the street, even though they're downtown at dinnertime on a sunny Friday. Paris of the Eighties, indeed.

"You his mother?" says the guy.

"What if I was?" she says. Jeffrey Tunxis now has his hands folded into bony fists. He's clearly decided he'd rather fight and die than have Kate dig any further into whatever this is.

"Fuck you, you're his mother," the guy says to her. "You were just standing here."

"Fuck you right back, buster," says Kate. She adjusts the keys in her hand. "Is this what you do? You pick on younger kids and ladies? Tough guy?" She can feel her pulse throbbing in her neck. Oh, the motherhood is flowing now.

"Just quit it, okay?" says Jeffrey Tunxis.

The guy smiles. "Anyone ask you to speak, pussy boy?" He gives Tunxis' chest a shove. To Kate, he says, "If you're his mother, then you should know this boy likes to suck strange dick at the movies."

"Really?" says Kate. "Because I was in that movie. You're *loud,* Mr. Balcony." The guy's face goes slack. Jeffrey Tunxis is *really* not looking at her now.

White Tank-Top lets go of Tunxis and steps past him to loom over Kate. "I'm gonna give you three to get out of here," he says. "One."

Kate holds up her fist. Her car key—the longest, most jagged of the bunch—is extended like a spike between her fingers. From the three weeks of single-lady self-defense classes she took at the YWCA, this is the one thing she remembers: Keep your sharpest key between your fingers. Walk at night with your keys like this, the instructor said, and your potential attacker will see you're more trouble than you're worth. Fine advice, but right now she wishes she had some of Miles' homemade weaponry with her.

Kate's potential attacker giggles at her. "Two," he says.

"I won't be able to stop you," says Kate. "But I'm going to take an eye with me. Or an eardrum. Or a cheek. All three, maybe." She hopes all this doesn't sound as shuddery as it feels.

"Three," counts the guy. They both stand there, his hands slack at his sides, her fist in the air between them. She can feel Jeffrey Tunxis staring.

The guy swings his hand up and chucks her on the chin: lightly, like a playful uncle might. Kate flinches, but does not move her fist from where it is. Then Mr. Balcony turns and glares at Tunxis. "Don't ever faggot in here again," he says, and he walks off. Kate grabs Jeffrey Tunxis' arm and pulls him the other way, toward the crosswalk.

Tunxis rides in the back of her Datsun, looking out the window, swallowing the passing houses with his enormous eyes. They're just out of Worcester now. There are still twenty more minutes to his house. Two hours ago, she hated him, this kid. Now she can't. What must this be like, having to constantly armor yourself against what you really are? Going from breakfast with a father like his, to unzipping your other life in a dark movie theater? It's shocking to learn a person like this has depth. Suddenly she wants to give him—what's it called?—support.

"What is it with men, huh?" says Kate. "You do for them the one thing they *all* want, and then what? Once they're finished up, you're dogshit." She breathes deeply, surprised at her energy and audacity. Her lungs are tingling. There hasn't been anyone else to say this kind of thing to. Most of the women she knows are still trying to pretend marriage is the best thing that ever happened to them. Or that divorce is. No one on either side will hedge their bets enough to admit that men are all little bullies in big bodies. She should reach out to Jeffrey Tunxis, that's what she should do. Take him to a meeting for secret gay kids or something.

In the rearview mirror, Jeffrey Tunxis is so coiled and red-faced and clenched that he looks like he's trying to strangle himself with isometrics.

"What?" says Kate. "Did I say some—"

"You didn't see shit," he says. He sounds almost like his attacker. In the rearview mirror, Tunxis stares at her and shakes his head slowly. *No.*

And that's it. No plea to not tell anyone, no stuttering explanation for what they both know happened today, no bold declaration of his sexuality. She is expected to shut up and forget everything. This kid will never acknowledge her, she knows, will never be any nicer to Miles: Possibly he'll be meaner, even. Either way, he'll just go on doing what he's doing. Maybe he'll beat up some freshman in gym class on Monday. In May, he'll probably take some knockout from another town to all the formals. Then, after graduation, he'll be gone, living a fun new life with no thought for the people he shit on because he couldn't handle his old one. Or else he'll stay around and knock up the knockout, just to prove to himself that he can.

And to think: Kate was there to help make a defining moment in this young man's life.

It's 6:50, later than she'd thought. They're nearly to Tunxis' house, but Miles will be shambling out to the sidewalk at Clark soon, looking for his mother's car. She can picture him, he who's not had his mouth on anyone else's body since infancy, standing out there in his homemade chain mail and sweatpants. And where is Mom, his only protector in the world? Out chauffeuring one of his chief tormentors. Kate LaPine knows this is not the stuff of Mother of the Year.

She swerves into a Texaco parking lot and swings the car around in a U.

"Jesus, what now?" says Jeffrey Tunxis.

"We're going to pick up Miles."

"Just drop me here, then. I'll walk." He reaches for the door handle. There's an empty space in the traffic, and Kate stomps on the gas. Tunxis lurches backward in his seat. He glares at her and mutters something she's pretty sure is "kidnapping." Kate ignores him.

"We'll say you ran out of bus money," she says, "and you were about to call your folks when I happened to spot you from my car."

"We'll say to who?"

"To Miles. You're going to get out and open his door for him. Then you're going to talk to him for at least half the ride home. You don't have to talk about Dungeons and Dragons. As his mother, that's my particular cross to bear. And you don't have to be all buddy-buddy, except for the door-opening. Just be *decent* to him. Tonight and for the rest of high school."

"There's no way. I'm sorry, but he's gross and weird. Everyone thinks so."

"Really? Would you have the balls to walk around wearing chain mail?"

He laughs. "I wouldn't *have* chain mail. See? He puts himself in that position."

"You're one to talk about positions, kid."

He leans forward, squinting at her. "Now I'm definitely not doing what you want."

"Fine. Then I'll do all the talking—starting tonight, when I get home to my telephone. Lot of mothers I haven't spoken to in a while. Who's your buddy on the soccer team, that Wozniak kid? His mom cuts my hair. Let's see: Ed Bemis' mother, Mark Sandstrum's. All the moms sure do like you. And all their sons know you, right, Jeffrey? But how *well* do they know you?" And Jeffrey Tunxis is quiet and small again, much like when she first saw him outside today. He shrinks down in his seat and goes back to looking out the window. He does not look very defiant.

She's just reserved herself a coach-class seat to Hell, she knows, but hey: How many opportunities do you get to improve the life of your teenaged son, even marginally? She can't get him laid, but maybe she can make his life a little easier. Kate has always known she'd kill for her children, but how often we overlook *maiming*.

Somewhere in her bedroom closet is a little plastic statue Miles gave her for Mother's Day, the year he was five. It's a pink dragon with long eyelashes, hugging a small blue dragon to her chest. On the base, it says *World's Beast Mom*. Kate makes a note to dig it out when they get home. That fucker needs to go out on the kitchen counter, where people can see it.